AMNESIA

Also by LJ Ross

THE ALEXANDER GREGORY THRILLERS

1. Impostor
2. Hysteria
3. Bedlam
4. Mania
5. Panic
6. Amnesia

THE DCI RYAN MYSTERIES

1. Holy Island
2. Sycamore Gap
3. Heavenfield
4. Angel
5. High Force
6. Cragside
7. Dark Skies
8. Seven Bridges
9. The Hermitage
10. Longstone
11. The Infirmary (Prequel)
12. The Moor
13. Penshaw
14. Borderlands
15. Ryan's Christmas
16. The Shrine
17. Cuthbert's Way
18. The Rock
19. Bamburgh
20. Lady's Well
21. Death Rocks
22. Poison Garden
23. Belsay
24. Berwick

THE SUMMER SUSPENSE MYSTERIES

1. The Cove
2. The Creek
3. The Bay
4. The Haven

AMNESIA

AN ALEXANDER GREGORY THRILLER

LJ ROSS

PENGUIN BOOKS

PENGUIN BOOKS

UK | USA | Canada | Ireland | Australia
India | New Zealand | South Africa

Penguin Books is part of the Penguin Random House group of companies
whose addresses can be found at global.penguinrandomhouse.com

Penguin Random House UK,
One Embassy Gardens, 8 Viaduct Gardens, London SW11 7BW

penguin.co.uk

First published in 2024 by LJ Ross
Published in Penguin Books 2026
001

Copyright © LJ Ross, 2024

The moral right of the author has been asserted

This is a work of fiction. Names, characters, businesses, places,
events and incidents are either the products of the author's
imagination or used in a fictitious manner. Any resemblance to actual
persons, living or dead, or actual events is purely coincidental.

Penguin Random House values and supports copyright. Copyright fuels creativity, encourages diverse voices, promotes freedom of expression and supports a vibrant culture. Thank you for purchasing an authorised edition of this book and for respecting intellectual property laws by not reproducing, scanning or distributing any part of it by any means without permission. You are supporting authors and enabling Penguin Random House to continue to publish books for everyone. No part of this book may be used or reproduced in any manner for the purpose of training artificial intelligence technologies or systems. In accordance with Article 4(3) of the DSM Directive 2019/790, Penguin Random House expressly reserves this work from the text and data mining exception.

Printed and bound in Great Britain by Clays Ltd, Elcograf S.p.A.

The authorised representative in the EEA is Penguin Random House Ireland,
Morrison Chambers, 32 Nassau Street, Dublin D02 YH68

A CIP catalogue record for this book is available from the British Library

ISBN: 978–1–804–96049–3

Penguin Random House is committed to a sustainable future
for our business, our readers and our planet. This book is made
from Forest Stewardship Council® certified paper.

CHAPTER 1

South London, 1995

Daniel Nkosi had big dreams.

He dreamed of becoming a premiership football player, and of buying his mum and dad a nice house in the suburbs. He dreamed of putting his little sister through university, since she was the brainy one of the bunch, and of having a nice family of his own, one day. He could see it now: big, raucous barbeques on sunny days, with plenty of laughter, singing and dancing.

The best part?

Those dreams might be possible.

A scout from Tottenham FC was coming to watch his game the following weekend, and another one from Arsenal the weekend after.

If he kept his form and stayed focused, it could be his chance.

All he needed was a chance.

"Daniel!"

He looked up at the sound of his coach's booming voice, coming at him from the other end of the floodlit astroturf.

"Gather up those balls, Danny!"

He nodded, and stopped stretching out his hamstrings so that he could begin scooping up the stray footballs that had found their way to the edge of the pitch. The other members of his team were gathering up their things and he waved to them as they trailed off, exhausted but happy, as he was.

Presently, his coach joined him and took a couple of the balls from his hands. "You played well tonight," he said, as they made their way back to the clubhouse. "Keep working on your tactical awareness ahead of next weekend's game, and I think you've got it made, son."

Phil Duggan was a man in his sixties, who'd inherited a love of the Beautiful Game from his father and his grandfather before him, both of whom had been lifelong West Ham supporters. He was a proud Hammer himself, and onetime member of their youth team, until injury had killed off that particular future with one vicious kick to the Achilles. It had taken years to come to terms with the loss of what could have been, but, once he had, he'd found solace and a sense of purpose working with the young lads whose future was still unwritten. He helped them to become better footballers and, perhaps more importantly, helped to keep them off the streets and out of the gangs which were an omnipresent scourge in that part of London.

Very occasionally, he came across a player who had a real chance of making it, which brought a little ripple of excitement. He loved to see them flourish and develop, to hone their skills alongside their discipline, and to wonder whether, one day, they'd wear a sacred yellow and maroon jersey as he watched them from the stands.

Daniel Nkosi was one such kid.

At fourteen, he was already older than most of the young players who entered the premiership youth academies. He'd discovered the game too late, but had shown a natural talent from the outset and over the course of the past two years had continued to shine so it was possible—just *possible*—that he could still make it.

"I'll do my best, coach," he said, and Phil gave him an encouraging pat on the back.

"I know you will," he said. "You're a good kid, Daniel. No matter what happens, I'm proud of the work you've put in."

The boy's smile lit up his whole face.

"Better be on your way home," Phil said, with an eye for the time. "It's getting late."

Beyond the floodlights of the football pitch, the sun had disappeared over the horizon and the streets of London glowed murky orange as the streetlamps flickered into life.

"It's just around the corner," Daniel reminded him. "Are you sure you don't want me to give you a hand?"

Phil smiled.

A good kid.

"That's all right. I'll see you next Saturday—stay out of trouble until then."

Daniel nodded, and tugged a black fleeced hoodie over his head to keep himself warm. Now that the pleasant ache of a ninety-minute game had worn off, the air was cool against his skin, and he was looking forward to a hot shower and a bite to eat. "Bye!" he called out, slinging his rucksack over his shoulder.

"Mind as you go," Phil said, absent-mindedly. As he closed up the clubhouse doors, he looked back at the teenage boy who was the greatest hope their club had seen in a decade, and felt an odd flutter of panic in his chest.

As if somebody had walked over his grave.

He opened his mouth to call to Daniel, then stopped himself. "Imaginin' things," Phil muttered, and closed off the lights.

Daniel set off on the ten-minute journey home from the sports ground, a plastic bag swinging from his hand containing the new boots he'd been given for his birthday. The streets were quiet at that time, most people having settled into their homes for the evening or otherwise enjoying themselves at one of the pubs or clubs scattered across the city. He hummed a tune beneath his breath, something he'd heard at church the previous Sunday, about God having made all things bright and beautiful. There, amidst the litter-lined streets and the graffiti-tarnished walls of London, he felt it was true.

The world *was* bright and beautiful.

Especially the welcoming lights of Mr Ali's Corner Shop, which beckoned as he approached the estate where his family lived. Fishing a few coins from his pocket, Daniel pushed open the door, which jingled a merry tune, and stepped inside the little emporium.

Mr Ali looked up from his inspection of a stock report, and, recognising the boy, smiled cheerfully. "Hello there, Daniel. Been at football practice?"

"Yes, Mr Ali."

Always polite, he thought. "What can I get you, this time?"

Daniel considered his change. "I'll have a Lucozade," he said. "And a Turkish Delight for my sister."

Ali smiled to himself, and wondered how many of the other young thugs who came into his shop would have stopped to think of their siblings.

Not many.

"Here you are," he said. "Give my best to your mum and dad."

"Thanks, Mr Ali," Daniel said, and made his way back out into the night.

The shopkeeper watched his retreating back, and then turned up the volume on his little television set and settled down to watch the next episode of *Eastenders*.

Daniel had polished off most of his energy drink by the time he reached Xavier House. The u-shaped block of flats was nothing short of a concrete monstrosity, created sometime in the sixties to provide cheap social housing and then forgotten about in the decades that followed, much like its residents. The flats were accessed via a concrete walkway, which led into a large grassy quadrangle boasting a rusted set of swings and a few old benches, overlooked by a series of galleried balconies on each of the fifteen floors of the mid-rise building.

As he made his way along the walkway, Daniel found most of the lights had blown or been vandalised, so he walked a bit faster through the shadows, eager now to get home. His footsteps echoed around the walls, which carried a strong stench of stale urine and marijuana, and he wondered why the walkway seemed to grow longer every time he passed through it. Finally, he emerged into the quadrangle, where he breathed deeply of the chilly night air and then veered left, towards the southern entrance of the building where his family occupied a three-bedroom flat on the twelfth floor. As he passed one of the benches on the edge of the grass, he saw that it was occupied by a group of young, white men, whom he recognised immediately as being part of one of the local gangs.

He swore softly beneath his breath, and kept his head down.

Keep walking, he thought. *Just keep walking, and they might not notice you.*

"*Oi!* Daniel, innit?"

He kept walking, and pretended not to hear.

"C' mere, boy! We wanna talk to yer!"

Daniel's jaw clenched, and he couldn't prevent the automatic look of disdain that crossed his face, before he snapped his eyes back to the pavement.

It was all the ammunition they needed.

"*Oi!* Was you lookin' at me? Got somethin' to say, 'ave yer?"

Daniel watched three of them rise to their feet and then lope towards him across the darkened quad, aggression in every line of their bodies. His heart began to pound against the wall of his chest, and his eyes strayed to the entrance doors, which were still a couple of hundred metres away from where he stood.

"I didn't mean anythin' by it," he said, palms held up. "I'm sorry."

"You will be."

They surrounded him, and hard hands began to shove him back and forth, like a pinball.

"Stop—*stop* it—*please*—"

"Or what?" one of them snarled. "What're you gonna do, *boy*?"

In the brief seconds that followed, Daniel turned on his heel and ran, as fast as his legs could carry him.

It wasn't fast enough.

They were older, and their bodies were honed with lean muscle which they used without mercy. As the golden, welcoming light of the entrance came within Daniel's grasp, they caught him, knocking him to the floor so that he skidded against the worn tarmac and the skin ripped from his legs.

Then, they got to work.

Daniel felt the first brutal kick to his skull, even the second and the third, and heard them laughing, like hyenas.

After the fourth, he felt nothing.

He heard nothing.

They continued to stamp on his head and kick his vital organs, long after Daniel Nkosi had lost consciousness. Their vicious grunts, combined with maniacal laughter, disturbed one of the residents who eventually roused themselves from the television and wandered onto their balcony to call down into the murky shadows of the night.

"Hey! What's goin' on down there? *Clear off!*"

They did, scattering off into the night, their laughter ringing through the walkways.

Daniel lay there on the hard ground, his body twitching, a plastic bag still clutched in one hand, while the other stretched towards a bar of Turkish Delight which had landed in a puddle near his head.

The puddle was slowly filling with blood.

CHAPTER 2

A large crowd had gathered by the time the first police car turned up, its blue lights spinning a silent disco against the concrete walls of Xavier House. Detective Sergeant Richard Vaughn stepped out first, followed by a constable whose name he'd already forgotten, and they made their way across the quadrangle to see what all the fuss was about.

"All right, all right," he said, stifling a yawn. "Everybody move *back*!"

Once they'd cleared, he saw a boy of fourteen or fifteen lying face down on the tarmac path, his body unmoving. Even in the semi-darkness, it was obvious he'd suffered extreme trauma to the back of his skull, and had lost a significant amount of blood.

Vaughn moved forward and dropped to his haunches, to feel for a pulse.

Faint, he thought. *But still there.*

"What happened here?" he asked the crowd.

A man in his seventies spoke first. "He was attacked," he said. "I saw a gang of white boys crowdin' round 'im fifteen minutes ago, all laughin' and jokin'. They were givin' 'im a kickin' but they ran off, when I called out. They were all wearin' sports gear and one of them—the biggest one—had a scar across his face, I'm sure 'e did."

"You sure about that?" Vaughn asked him. "It's dark out here."

"My flat's only on the third floor," the old man replied, and turned to point. "I could see in the light of the entrance, 'ere, anyway. I got a good look at 'em."

Vaughn looked up at the entrance to the southern block, where a bright white industrial light beamed its rays onto the pathway, illuminating the boy's body.

He stood up and stepped away, pushing the crowd even further back.

"All right, show's over! Ambulance is already on its way. Constable? Take down the details of everyone who saw what happened. The rest of you, go back to your homes!"

They began to disperse, crying and muttering amongst themselves, and then, satisfied that his constable was otherwise engaged, Vaughn returned to the boy's body and made a show of checking for vital signs. With another swift glance over his shoulder, he palmed a small bag of hash from his inner breast pocket and slid it inside the boy's hoodie before standing up again.

A few minutes later, the constable re-joined him. "Shouldn't we check for ID?"

Vaughn gestured for him to go ahead, and waited patiently for the discovery to be made.

It didn't take long.

"Guv? Look at this!"

"What's that?"

The constable held up the bag of hash and they exchanged a telling glance. "I think we've found the motive," Vaughn said, and made a tutting sound. "Any ID on him?"

The constable rooted around Daniel's pockets and found a wallet, which contained his membership card for the sports ground he'd recently come from. "Daniel Nkosi," he read out.

Vaughn grunted.

Just then, they heard the sound of approaching sirens, and the ambulance crew appeared at the head of the walkway moments later. They came at a run, dragging bags of equipment with them and a portable stretcher, but they were too late. They were far too late.

Daniel was already dead.

Irene Nkosi was doing the washing up when she heard the dim sound of youths laughing in the quadrangle downstairs, from their twelfth floor flat. Leaning forward, she could see nothing from the kitchen window, which looked out at the north block on the other side, as a mirror image.

"James?" she called out.

Her husband had dozed off in one of the easy chairs in the lounge.

"*James!*"

He stirred, and rubbed his tired eyes. "What is it?" he called out.

"Something's going on downstairs," she called back.

"Don' worry 'bout it," he told her. "It'll be that gang of no-goods, same as usual."

Her lips flattened, and she dried her hands on a tea towel before heading out to the balcony to try to get a better look. She opened the old metal doors with a *whoosh*, letting a cold burst of air into the flat, and then peered over the concrete railing.

Far below, she could see a small crowd had gathered on the pathway. "Somethin's happened," she said, and stepped back inside.

"Well?" James asked.

"I can't see much, but there's a crowd down there," she said. "I hope there hasn't been another knife attack."

Irene crossed herself, and said a silent prayer for whichever family would grieve. Then, her eye caught the clock on the mantelpiece.

"Daniel's late home, tonight," she murmured, and a small worry began to fester in the pit of her stomach.

"He'll have stopped at the corner shop," James said, with another yawn. "You know what he's like."

She rubbed a hand over her arm, and nodded. "Yes," she said. "You're probably right."

But the festering feeling wouldn't go away, and only grew stronger as the minutes ticked by.

Half an hour later, a knock came at the door.

Irene stared at it for long seconds, and found herself frozen, unable to move from her seat.

"James—"

"Aye, I'll get it," he said, and roused himself.

He checked the peep hole, and frowned.

Police.

With a flicker of nerves, he undid the lock and pulled the door open to find two men standing there in badly fitting suits, both wearing the shark-eyed stares of non-uniform police.

"Mr Nkosi?"

"Yes," he replied. "Can I help you?"

"I'm DI Lipman, and this is DS Vaughn," the elder of the two said, with a slight Liverpudlian twang. "Can we come in?"

"Do you have any identification, please?"

As a black immigrant in London, James had been stopped and searched more times than he cared to recall, and without any good reason. He had a justifiable wariness of the police, and had learned to operate around them with extreme caution.

Obviously irritated, they retrieved their warrant cards for his inspection.

"Thank you—come in, please."

He stood aside to allow them to precede him, and Irene came to her feet.

"Mrs Nkosi?"

Judging from their expressions, they were obviously surprised to find she was pale skinned, in contrast to her husband. Irene was used to the reaction, but it never failed to disappoint.

"What's happened?" she whispered.

Lipman exchanged a glance with Vaughn, and then adopted a sympathetic expression. "We're very sorry to tell you that your son, Daniel, has died," he said. "You have our sympathies."

The words were perfunctory.

Irene's legs gave way, and she sank back onto the chair as all colour drained from her face.

"I—I don' understand what you're sayin'," James said, and moved across the room to put a hand on his wife's shoulder. "There mus' be some mistake."

"There's no mistake, Mr Nkosi. Daniel was found with serious head injuries, and, despite our best efforts, he was pronounced dead at the scene."

"The—the scene?" James whispered. "What *scene*? What're you talkin' about?"

"Downstairs," Irene whispered. "The crowd downstairs. It was for Daniel. It was for *Daniel*—"

She began to rock in her chair, while silent tears coursed down her cheeks.

"Where is he?" James asked them. "Where's my boy?"

"Daniel has been taken to hospital," Lipman replied. "We'll be glad to take you there, so you can make a formal identification."

Irene let out a low, wailing sound, like an animal in torment.

"Who—who did this thing?" James asked, swiping tears from his own eyes. "Who killed him?"

The officers exchanged another glance.

"It's too early to say," Vaughn replied, staring somewhere over his left shoulder. "We'll be investigating over the coming days."

"Why?" James asked, brokenly. "*Why?*"

Vaughn scratched the side of his chin. "Mr Nkosi, I'm sorry to have to ask you this, but…we found drugs on your son's body. A bag of hash. Do you know anything about that?"

"*What?*" Irene almost shouted, as anger momentarily overruled devastation. "Daniel would never touch drugs. He's a good boy…"

She began to weep, and James held her against him. "Irene's right," he said, firmly. "Daniel would be the last to touch that filthy stuff."

Lipman ran his tongue over his lips. "What about if he was moving it for someone?" he suggested. "Or looking after it for a friend? He might not have been a user himself, but it's possible he fell in with the wrong crowd. Do you know who he spent time with?"

Irene was too overwrought to speak, so James drew himself in and tried to think.

"Daniel has a close circle," he said. "They're all good kids, from good families. We attend the same church, and the boys sing in the choir together. They've known each other since they were born."

He gave their names and addresses, which Vaughn took down without much enthusiasm.

"What about any new acquaintances?"

"He hasn't spoken about anyone," James said. "Daniel knows to keep himself to himself, and stay away from the wrong element. He's an intelligent boy."

"*Was*," Irene whispered. "He was."

James rubbed at his eyes again, and turned away to look out of the window.

Then, he spun back around.

"Why you askin' all these questions about Daniel and his friends, anyway?" he demanded. "You should be out there, findin' out who killed 'im!"

"We will, Mr Nkosi, we will," Lipman said. "Would you mind if we had a look at his room, while we're here? We might find something helpful."

Vaughn thought of the other bag of hash he had in his pocket, and wondered where to plant it.

"Yes, *I mind*!" Irene said, coming to her feet. "I want to see my boy! I want whoever—whatever *animal* killed him to be found! I don't want you proddin' and pokin' around his things, as if—as if—he was some criminal! Get out! Just—get *out!*"

Lipman and Vaughn left details of the hospital where Daniel had been taken and decided to try again later, perhaps when the family weren't home. They let themselves out of the flat with a few more trite words of sympathy, and all that punctuated the empty silence that followed their departure was the sound of Irene's ragged tears.

"Mum?"

They looked up to see their ten-year-old daughter standing in the doorway wearing a frightened expression on her young face.

"What's happened to Daniel?"

Irene could only shake her head.

"Your brother's gone to Heaven, Ava," her father said. "He's—he's with the angels, now."

Ava watched her parents crumple, and, with a sharp cry, ran across the room to join them, burying herself between them as if that single act of solidarity could prevent her family being ripped apart at the seams.

CHAPTER 3

London, Present Day

Detective Chief Inspector Ava Hope awakened against a starched hospital pillow.

The bandage that had once covered most of her head had been removed and replaced with a smaller one, to protect the area where a bullet had entered and exited her left temporal lobe, grazing the hippocampus and taking most of her long-term memories with it. The wound still ached, and she raised a shaking hand to touch the spot, before letting it fall back against the bedsheets.

"How're you feeling today, boss?"

Surprised to find she wasn't alone, Ava turned and saw a man she recognised seated in one of the ugly visitors' chairs. He was enjoying a four-fingered Kit Kat with considerable relish and, beside him, a helium balloon bore the message, 'GET WELL SOON'.

"Carter," she said. "Are you trying to skive off work, again, by coming to visit me?"

Detective Sergeant Ben Carter, her partner in Major Crimes back at The Yard, let out a barking laugh which sprayed a small amount of chocolate wafer in her general direction. "Fact is, we've got a bet running in the office to see how quickly your memory comes back," he said. "I've laid odds on four-to-one it's before the end of the month, so I'm here to help you along the way."

Ava huffed out a laugh, and then closed her eyes as a fresh wave of pain rocketed through her system.

"Do you want me to call a nurse?" he offered. "You might be due some medication."

"It's okay, I've got a button here," she said, reaching for the line hanging nearby. "It gives me something if I need it, but I'm trying not to become reliant. It's good stuff."

She gave him a weak smile, which he returned.

"Probably wise," he said. "Oh, before I forget—"

He rose from his chair with a loud squeak against its pleather coating, and handed her an envelope.

"A few people back at The Yard wanted to send you their best wishes," he said. "Would you like some help opening it?"

In addition to severe memory loss, the brain injury had affected Ava's motor skills, which made walking a serious challenge as well as any other ordinary actions using her hands or arms.

"Let me try," she said. "The physiotherapist keeps telling me that I should challenge myself."

She held the envelope easily enough but, when it came to sliding her finger beneath the flap to open it, it took eight or nine attempts before she heard the first rip of paper. By then, she'd almost given in to weak tears.

"Well done," Carter said, and took his seat again. "I hope you don't mind me coming to visit unannounced. The doc said it would help to bring back your memory, if you saw some familiar faces."

Ava shook her head. "I don't mind," she said, setting the card on the bedside table. "Anything that helps me to remember my old life, and you to win your bet, is a good thing."

"Has anything come back to you, yet?" he asked.

She shook her head. "Not much," she said. "They tell me I've got retrograde amnesia, which means I've lost the memories I made shortly before my injury, rather than anterograde, which means I can still form new memories. I suppose I should be grateful for that."

She pointed towards a leatherbound journal sitting on the bedside table.

"I'm supposed to make a note of anything worth remembering," she explained. "Apparently, repetition helps to reinforce memories, and having them written down allows me to read them back any time I like."

His fingers itched to look inside, so he clasped them together.

"Unfortunately, just to make matters worse, the doctors say I'm also suffering from post-traumatic amnesia," she said. "The two combined means that I'm struggling to recall things from the past, and especially anything around the time of the injury. I can make new memories, but it feels sort of…rusty. That's to do with trauma, rather than amnesia. It's why I remember your face, but sometimes can't quite remember your name, even though I know you've come to visit me several times."

"Maybe I've just got one of those faces," he said, with a smile. "I blend in."

She considered him and supposed that was true; Ben Carter was a man in his early thirties and possessed of average, unremarkable features she might have seen walking along any street in London.

He'd have made a good spy, came the thought, out of nowhere.

She fiddled with the bedsheet. "At least I'm alive," she said, trying to focus on something positive. "Others aren't so lucky."

Carter raised an eyebrow. "Indeed," he murmured, thinking of one or two in particular.

"I'm told there was another woman—a doctor—who was injured at the same time as me," Ava said. "How is she doing?"

Something unreadable passed over Carter's face. "Naomi Palmer," he reminded her.

"Unfortunately, she's not faring as well as you. She was attacked with the butt of a weapon, but the position and force of the injury was more serious than being shot, in some ways."

Ava looked away. "I'm sorry to hear that. I wish I remembered her, since we were obviously in the same place at the same time, but I have no idea who she is."

Carter wondered. "I could show you a picture of her?" he offered.

Ava gnawed on her lip, and then nodded. "All right," she said. "It might jog something."

Carter retrieved his phone, scrolled for a second or two, and then held it up to her. "This is Doctor Palmer."

Ava found herself staring into the smiling eyes of a very beautiful, dark-haired woman dressed in a tailored red dress. Beneath her image was a block of text detailing a short biography of her education and professional history, which was impressive.

The thread of a memory tugged at the corners of her mind, an image of that woman seated beside her at a dining table eating pasta, then it frittered away.

"I don't remember," Ava said quietly, and turned away. "You've told me about her, of course, and the circumstances, but I don't remember anything of my own accord."

"Don't worry about it," Carter replied, easily. "You'd only met Naomi a couple of times, so it's not surprising you don't remember much about her—especially since she was there at the attack, and your mind has blocked that part out."

Ava nodded, and handed the phone back to him. "Thanks for coming to see me," she said. "You must be a good friend."

Carter gave her a bland smile. "You'd have done the same," he said. "Besides, the work's starting to pile up, back at The Yard. We need you to hurry up and recover, so you can get back to doing what you do best."

"Detective work?"

"Kicking our arses," he said, and made her laugh. Carter checked the time on his watch, and then rose to his feet. "I'd better start making tracks," he said.

"Thanks for coming, Ben—or do I call you Carter?"

"Depends on your mood," he said. "I don't mind either."

He made to leave, but she stopped him.

"*Wait*! This is an odd question, but, do you… do you happen to like cheese and onion crisps?"

"They're my favourite," he said. "Why?"

"I remembered," she said happily. "Maybe some things are starting to come back."

Carter looked at her, and wished he could see behind her eyes. "It's only a matter of time," he said, and raised a hand in farewell.

On another ward in the same hospital, Doctor Alexander Gregory took a disinterested sip of lukewarm coffee and watched the rhythmic rise and fall of Naomi's chest as she lay inert on the bed in front of him. She'd lost weight, despite the tube that fed her oesophagus and the line that kept her hydrated. Her skin was so pale it was almost grey, but the wound that had reduced her to a comatic state was no longer visible and, were it not for the mass of wires protruding from her veins, he might have thought she was merely sleeping.

A sleeping beauty.

Tears pricked the back of his eyes, and he rose from the chair to pace around, refusing to allow himself the indulgence. He'd cried, in those first few days, until he thought there were no more tears to shed, and yet the heartbreak returned each time he looked upon the woman he loved, and mourned all that could have been.

He turned back and forced himself to smile.

"The sun's shining today," he told her, and pulled his chair close to the bed, so that he could hold her hand. "I can't wait for you to wake up, Naomi. I'll show you all around London… wherever you want to go. We'll visit every bookshop in the city, if you like."

She'd spent much of her life in upstate New York, most recently as director of the exclusive Buchanan Institute, a private facility for those suffering with major psychiatric illnesses. He'd met her there while posing undercover as an inpatient, never expecting to fall in love with the woman tasked with helping him. They'd barely had any time together before Fate—

No, he thought.

Not Fate.

It hadn't been Fate who'd delivered the cruel blow to her head, but Carl Deere, a once-innocent man with sadistic tendencies who'd been driven mad by his own quest for vengeance. Naomi hadn't been part of his mission, she'd been an innocent bystander.

It made no sense, Gregory thought.

Carl Deere had murdered numerous people, but only those he perceived to have wronged him after playing some part in sending him to prison for crimes he hadn't committed. Carl's mission, or so he'd told himself, was to prevent other people from suffering similar injustice in the future. He had a code, of sorts, and only killed those who breached it.

But Naomi?

She hadn't been involved in Carl's wrongful imprisonment, and nor had DCI Hope. Neither woman deserved the brutality he'd shown them, and Gregory couldn't understand what had prompted the attacks—except that they'd happened to be in the wrong place, at the wrong time.

Perhaps that was all the explanation there was.

Gregory looked down at Naomi's hand, and brushed his fingers gently against her skin.

"We'll never know," he said aloud. "Carl's dead, so we'll never know why he did it."

Gregory watched her face for any flicker of movement, any sign of awareness, but found nothing.

He raised her hand to his lips, and kissed it.

"There's no rush, my love," he whispered. "Take all the time you need. I'll be waiting for you."

There was no reply, except for the intermittent *bleep* of the monitor.

CHAPTER 4

When Alex finally emerged from Naomi's room and made his way back down the long corridors of the hospital, he found DS Carter waiting for him in the entrance lobby.

"Doctor Gregory?"

He turned at the sound of his name, and forced the muscles of his face into a social smile. "Carter," he said. "Good to see you."

"Professor Douglas told me you'd be here," the other man explained, referring to Bill Douglas, Gregory's closest friend and mentor in the world of psychiatry. "How's Naomi?"

"No change," Alex said, brusquely. "How about Ava?"

Carter caught the haunted expression on the other man's face, and was sorry for it.

"She remembered my favourite crisps," he said, with a lopsided smile. "It's something."

Alex's interest was piqued, but then his face cleared. "You have crumbs on your lapel," he said, pointing to the spot. "And—no offence—but you're carrying a faint aroma of cheese and onion."

Carter laughed, and brushed the crumbs from his jacket. "I guess it wasn't a real memory, after all."

"Not necessarily," Gregory said. "Smells can be very triggering, so perhaps that's what helped her to remember the fact you like those crisps."

"It would have been more gratifying if she'd remembered my stellar detective skills, but I suppose remembering something is better than nothing," Carter said. "The doctors say she isn't making much progress, even though it's been over a month now."

"Four weeks isn't that long," Gregory averred, although it felt like a lifetime. "How's her motor function?"

"Still patchy," Carter replied. "She opened an envelope today, after a few attempts, but she's still struggling to walk unaided."

Gregory had visited Ava a few times but, he was ashamed to say, not during the past week. His thoughts were all for Naomi, and the silent prison she lived in beneath the broken shell of her body. He hated to be apart from her, in case she was alone when she decided to wake up again, and he was determined to do all he could to speak to her and try to coax her mind back to reality. That being said, he needed to sleep and eat, and occasionally see other people, or he would be unfit for purpose.

"I'll look in on Ava, before I leave," he decided.

"I was going to ask if you would," Carter said, with some relief. "I've been going in, so has her mum and a few others from The Yard, because familiar faces are supposed to help. But…" He gave a frustrated shrug. "It doesn't seem to be doing much, and her family can't afford to send her to a private facility. The doctors and nurses have done a wonderful job here, but they're stretched." He spread his hands. "I know you've got a lot on your plate, worrying about Naomi and all, but I don't know who else to ask. You're the best, and that's what she needs to unlock her mind. It's what you do—you and Professor Douglas."

Gregory expelled a long sigh. "If you're asking me to treat her, I can't do that, Ben. For a start, I'm not practising at the moment," he said. "Even if I were, I'm prohibited on ethical grounds from beginning a dual relationship; that means I can't work with family or friends, and Ava is my friend."

Gregory had broken that rule before, and paid the price for it.

But Carter was undeterred.

"*Unofficially*, then," he said. "Talk to her as a friend who happens to be a psychiatrist."

Gregory shook his head again.

"Look," Carter said. "Ava put her neck out for you, when she offered to drive Naomi north and take her to safety. That's how the pair of them ended up crossing paths with Carl Deere, which might never have happened otherwise. The least you could do is see if you can help her to remember who she is."

Gregory couldn't argue the truth of that, but was surprised by the force of its delivery.

As for Carter, he wasn't proud of the lengths he had to go to, sometimes, but reminded himself it was all in pursuit of the greater good. He'd been as patient as he could be, waiting for Ava Hope to remember herself and be discharged from hospital. But, as the weeks wore on without any progress, he'd begun to wonder whether it was all an act, and if she was hiding behind her diagnosis to buy herself more time.

He wouldn't put it past her.

In fact, he wouldn't put *anything* past her.

For a number of years, he'd worked undercover as a member of the Metropolitan Police's so-called 'Ghost Squad', in pursuit of bent coppers within the organisation. He'd befriended DCI Hope, laughed in the canteen, shared jokes, tears, arguments and everything else on a daily basis as her right-hand man. He'd taken orders and made himself indispensable so that she would trust him implicitly, while he kept her under surveillance and came to understand her routines. He'd tried to draw her out on multiple occasions, without success, and, thus far, there was no evidence that could be levied against her.

But he *knew*.

Carter knew in his gut that Ava Hope was bent, the same way he'd known all the other times and in all the other investigations over the course of his career. He'd never been wrong before, and he wasn't wrong now. He just needed proof, and that was where Doctor Gregory came in. If she was faking it, then he'd surely be able to tell and, if she wasn't, then he'd help her to remember. She'd remember the faces of the people she'd killed, and, although she'd never admit it, she'd return to work, and his investigation could continue rather than remaining in limbo.

Unless—

Unless Ava already remembered she was a killer.

If she did, then she was infinitely more dangerous, especially once she could walk again.

Gregory made his way upstairs to the four-person ward where Ava had been an in-patient for the past few weeks. As the soles of his shoes squeaked against the linoleum floor, he thought of Southmoor, the special, maximum-security hospital that housed some of their country's most acutely unwell and dangerous criminals. As one of the psychiatrists there, he'd dealt with their most difficult cases, including his own mother, and had never been afraid of the clinical environment.

But now...

Now, fear of hospitals was beginning to seep into his bones, and he felt it, crawling over his skin like tentacles. He smelled illness and death, disinfectant and canteen food. He saw families in tears—doctors likewise—and heard their quiet sobs on the stairwells. He recognised it all, in one broad spectrum, and was part of their number. He'd cried on the same stairs; he'd eaten the same gloopy lasagne and stared at the same magnolia-painted walls. He'd gone to the chapel and prayed to a God he didn't believe in, just in case he was wrong, because he was afraid, just like everyone else. He was afraid of losing the person he loved, and of the life they might have had.

But he couldn't allow the fear to show, and his training helped with that. He detached himself, and donned a professional mask that allowed him to smile at the children he sometimes saw without hair on their heads, or the old man with liver spots dragging a trolley drip behind him. He smiled for their benefit, because they were braver than he was, and deserved strength rather than pity. For the same reasons, he summoned a smile as he approached Ava's ward, and it was firmly in place when he entered the room.

"Hello," he said, brightly. "Do you feel up to having a visitor?"

"Hi, Alex," she said, straightening up in her bed, which was on the right-hand side, nearest the door. "Of course, come in and pull up a chair."

"I'm sorry it's been a few days since I last came to see you," he began, after settling himself. "I'm afraid the weeks are rolling into each other, at the moment."

"Don't apologise," she said. "Carter told me about Naomi…I'm so sorry."

He looked down at his restless hands. "She just needs time," he said. "But, let's talk about you and your recovery. How are you feeling?"

"I'm a bit stronger than I was," she said. "A week or two ago, I wouldn't have been able to pull myself up to a seated position in bed, but I've been working on it and now I can."

"That's great," he said. "How about your memory?"

She rubbed an unsteady hand over her eyes. "It's like a vault, and I don't know the combination to unlock it."

He leaned back in his chair, and crossed one leg over the other. "Would you like some help from a friend?"

Ava looked into his eyes, which were a bold, emerald green and filled with a sadness that was fathoms deep. She wished she could remember more of their friendship prior to her injury, but could easily understand how she had come to like this quiet, patient man with a compassionate heart.

"What if I don't like what I remember?" she asked him.

"We all have memories we'd rather forget," he said, gently. "It's part of the fabric of life. There'll be a mixture of good and bad, which you should be prepared for, but try to remember it's the same for everyone. In your case, having worked as a murder detective, it's possible you may remember all kinds of things concerning past cases you've dealt with. That might be traumatic, but we can work through it together."

Buoyed by the prospect, she did something she hadn't done in a long while.

She decided to trust him.

"When do we begin?"

He smiled. "We already have."

CHAPTER 5

When Alex left the hospital, the sun had fallen off the edge of the Earth, leaving the skies a deep, midnight blue. The streets bustled with festive crowds making the most of the season, but, to his jaded eyes, the Christmas lights were a garish reminder of everything Naomi would miss that year.

He eschewed a taxi or public transport and began to walk briskly along the South Bank of the river towards his apartment building in an area known as 'Shad Thames', enjoying the feel of the December air against his skin, and the rush of blood to his muscles after a day spent indoors. He passed by restaurants and bars heaving with people enjoying a drink after work, or a bite to eat with friends, and felt voyeuristic. For many years, his workmates had been the clinical team at Southmoor Hospital, all of whom had been as eager as he was to return to their homes at the end of a gruelling day within its confines. As for any other friends, he supposed that left only Bill Douglas and, more recently, Ava Hope. The former had been a constant in his life, hovering somewhere between a father figure and a best friend, but Bill lived in Cambridge, where he taught the next generation about matters of the mind from his base at Hawking College. As for Ava, their friendship had been derailed by recent events, but he cared for her wellbeing and wanted her to make a full recovery—for her own sake, as well as the public she served. He did not invest in new friendships, as a general rule, which was a hangover from his childhood. He'd learned never to become too close to people, either as friends or as romantic attachments, because then you would never be hurt or disappointed. He'd never encountered any difficulty in meeting prospective partners, but neither had he ever felt compelled to enter into a meaningful or long-term commitment with any of them, which was undoubtedly because he harboured a deep-rooted mistrust of women thanks to his mother. When your primary caregiver killed two of your siblings and tried to kill you as well, it tended to create a complex that was hard to shift.

Naomi was different.

He'd felt it the first time they met, two years earlier in the Catskills Mountains. He'd tried to pinpoint exactly what made the difference; to understand why his reaction to her had been so different from all the other women he'd met over the years. He could have cited any number of personal qualities but, in truth, it came down to something far simpler.

They were a match.

Alex stuck his hands in the pockets of his overcoat and turned away from the couples who walked hand-in-hand along the riverbank, not wanting to think of Naomi, nor of the guilt he felt in leaving her alone. Most nights, when he managed to sleep, he found himself dreaming that she was beside him. When he awakened, it was to find reality was very different, and the grief hit him like a fist to the face. The worst of it was in knowing there was nothing—*absolutely nothing*—he could do to change things, or to hurry her recovery.

If she recovered, his mind whispered.

He continued to place one foot in front of the other, wandering along the river until the restaurants and bars gave way to a series of high-end residential buildings converted from old Victorian warehouses. He let himself into one of them and leaned against the wall of the lift as it chugged upstairs. His stomach rumbled loudly to remind him that it had been some time since he last ate, but the likelihood of there being any food in the fridge was remote.

It didn't matter.

Wearily, he slotted his key in the door and opened it.

The first thing he noticed was a strong smell of cooked meat and garlic, followed by the sound of pots and pans clattering around the kitchen. He looked across at the coat pegs and noticed a mid-length raincoat in a fetching shade of olive green, which hadn't been there when he'd left that morning.

Bill, he thought.

His friend had a spare key to the apartment, so he could use it to stay overnight whenever he was in town. Despite his exhaustion, Alex felt his spirits rise at the prospect of good company and, if he wasn't very much mistaken, a good meal as well.

He followed his nose along the corridor.

"Alex?" Bill called out. "Is that you?"

After recent events, they were both nervous about the prospect of unexpected guests, and he stepped into the open-plan living space to catch Bill replacing one of the larger chopping knives into the block on the kitchen counter.

"Only me," he said.

After noting the grey pallor to his friend's skin and the general air of exhaustion he carried with him, Bill stepped forward to embrace him. "Thought I'd surprise you," he said, after they drew apart again. "You're feeling a bit thin."

Alex couldn't argue with that. "I've been forgetting to eat," he admitted, and Bill made a murmuring sound of disapproval.

"Luckily for you, I've cooked for the five thousand."

Alex surveyed the kitchen, which boasted three steaming trays containing lasagne, some sort of curry and what he'd guess was moussaka.

"How many people are we expecting?"

Bill gave him a fatherly smile. "I anticipated you wouldn't have been looking after yourself," he said. "I thought you could freeze the rest, or put it in the fridge and eat it over the next few days."

Alex didn't know why that simple kindness should be the thing to reduce him to tears, but he struggled to hold them back.

"Wine?" he said, to distract himself. "I could open a bottle of red."

Bill understood the value of patience in drawing people out.

"Fill 'em up," he said, and reached for two wine glasses from the open shelf.

Once they'd seated themselves and taken the first few bites of what was—it had to be said—a superlative moussaka, conversation picked up again.

"Any news on Naomi?" Bill asked quietly.

Alex swallowed, and pushed his plate away, no longer able to stomach food. "Nothing worth telling," he replied, and knocked back a long gulp of wine. "The doctors re-assessed Naomi yesterday, using the Glasgow Coma Scale. She's still scoring pretty low, which doesn't bode well."

"Remind me what the scale covers?"

"Eye opening, verbal and voluntary movements in response to a command," Alex said, keeping his eyes fixed on the wine glass. "The lower the score on each, the higher the chance she's suffered a more severe brain injury."

"Has there been any change in her score?"

"Her eyes opened spontaneously the other day, according to the nurses on the ward," Alex replied.

"That's good—" Bill started to say.

"But there's been no response to any commands," Alex interrupted him. "*Nothing*, Bill, not even a flicker." He scrubbed at his eyes, and started to clear away their plates to give himself an occupation, but Bill stopped him.

"These can wait," he said, and put a hand over his. "I'm worried about Naomi, but I'm also worried about you, Alex. You can't go on like this."

"Like what?" Gregory asked. "Like a man who's had his heart carved out of his chest? Like a man completely eaten away with guilt?"

"Yes," Bill replied. "Just like that."

Alex pushed away from the table and began pacing around the floor. "Every moment I'm away from her, I worry that'll be the time she wakes up, or—or..." He drew in a quivering breath. "Or the time she dies."

"The doctors have said she's stable, haven't they?"

"Yes, but there's no predicting these things," Alex muttered. "You and I both know conditions like hers can change overnight."

Bill nodded. "That's true," he was forced to admit. "But, Alex, listen to me. *It wouldn't be your fault*. It won't be *anyone's* fault, except the person who hurt Naomi."

Alex thought of Carl Deere, and his hands curled into fists. "There'll be no justice for her, whether she wakes up or not. He's dead."

Bill could hardly forget, since they'd both been present when Carl died. "You have to let go of the anger," he said. "It'll tear you apart."

Alex nodded, and unclenched his fists.

"I know," he muttered. "But still, it doesn't remove the feeling of impotence. We'll never know why he attacked Naomi and Ava, and stepped outside of his own mission to do it. I can't stop thinking about it, because it makes no sense."

Privately, Bill had pondered the same thing, but theorising wouldn't provide an answer.

"It's natural you should feel that way," he replied. "It's your job to help people, and try to make them better. You're faced with a situation in which you can't do either of those things."

Alex moved to the window, and stared unseeingly at the lights on the other side of the river.

"I keep thinking, if I see Naomi each day and talk to her, it'll make a difference."

"It might," Bill said.

"Or I might be fooling myself."

"Keep heart," his friend said. "You have to stay hopeful, until there's a reason not to."

Alex's lips twisted into a smile. "Speaking of hope, I saw Ava today," he said, and wandered over to the sofa across the room, where he allowed himself to collapse. "She's doing well, all things considered."

"That's wonderful news," Bill said. "Isn't it?"

Alex nodded, and ran a hand through his hair. "Her sergeant had a word with me today," he said. "Carter asked me to work with her, as a friend. He's concerned she isn't getting focused care because the staff at the hospital are overworked, and she needs a specialist."

"So, you, being the person you are, said yes?" Bill surmised.

Alex blew out a long sigh, and nodded. "He caught me at a vulnerable moment," he said. "I'd just come from seeing Naomi and, I suppose, I thought, if I can't help her, perhaps I could help Ava."

Bill took the chair opposite and listened.

"I don't want to make the same mistake I did last time," Alex continued. "I know it was wrong to treat my own mother—"

"That was a very unique situation," Bill pointed out.

"That may be true, but Ava was—*is*—a friend," he said.

"Yes, but you've already made it very clear you're not intending to treat her in any formal sense," Bill said. "It's true that you can't divorce yourself from the skills you have, or the tendency to use those skills in any given moment, but that would be the case even if Ava hadn't suffered acute memory loss. If she was simply asking you for relationship advice on a Tuesday afternoon, you'd approach it with a history of clinical experience, without even being aware of it."

Alex nodded.

"Besides," Bill said. "It could be a very interesting case, and you need the distraction."

He removed his glasses and began to polish them with the edge of his shirt.

"In any event," he said. "We don't have people beating a pathway to our door for our criminal profiling expertise, at the moment."

"We were completely cleared of all blame in Carl Deere's suicide," Gregory said, referring to the coroner's report which had come through the week before.

"Yes, but he died in the very office where our criminal profiling unit is based," Bill said, and pulled an expressive face. "It's hardly what any of us would have wanted, and it doesn't look good from the PR side of things, does it?"

There was no time to formulate a reply before Bill's mobile phone began to shrill from the pocket of his coat, in the hallway.

"I wonder who that could be at this hour," he said, and made a dash for it.

Alex was lost in thought when he returned, wearing an expression that was both curious and concerned. "Who is it?" he mouthed.

Bill held up a hand. "Yes—yes, I understand," he said, in serious tones. "And this happened when, exactly?"

There was a pause, during which Alex strained to hear the voice at the other end of the line.

"Of course. We'll be there first thing in the morning. Yes—goodbye."

Bill ended the call and when he looked up, his face was sombre. "Turns out I was wrong," he said. "There's still a demand for criminal profiling, after all."

Alex leaned forward. "What's happened?"

"The son of an MP has been kidnapped," Bill said. "He's only eight years old. He went missing earlier this evening and his parents received an e-mail a couple of hours later demanding online payment in bitcoin. It's government policy not to negotiate with terrorists or hostage-takers, so they need our help to bring him home."

Alex thought of Naomi, and of the time he'd be away from her bedside.

Then, he thought of a terrified young boy.

There was only one right thing to do.

CHAPTER 6

The multi-storey car park was almost empty by the time Carter entered on foot, his new shoes pinching his toes and rubbing the back of his heels. He made directly for the stairwell and ignored the dilapidated lift in favour of the concrete stairs which, although ancient, could at least be relied upon. He wheezed his way upward to the fifth floor and told himself that, this year, he'd stick to his New Year's resolution and go back to the gym.

When he reached the fifth floor, he scanned the parking area with a careful eye.

A few cars, he thought. *No sign of any other life.*

He walked directly towards one of the bays in the middle of the floor, where a black Volvo SUV was parked. As he approached, its headlights flashed once, and he quickened his pace.

Reaching the passenger door, he pulled it open and slipped inside, closing it softly behind him.

"You're late," the driver said.

"Sorry, I was held up."

"Well? What's the latest?"

"No change, apparently," Carter said. "She's either telling the truth about her amnesia, or she's a great actress."

The driver took a sip of coffee from a takeaway cup. "What do you think?"

Carter looked out of the blackened side window into the shadowed car park with its flickering overhead lights, and thought of the woman he knew as Ava Hope, but whose real name was Ava Nkosi.

"She's still my prime suspect," he said. "The reasons why we added her to the watchlist haven't changed; she had a deep-rooted motive for wanting Lipman and Vaughn dead."

"But there's still no evidence," the driver said. "You've worked by her side for almost three years now, and still haven't brought me a scrap of evidence to support your theory."

"She isn't a fool," Carter replied. "Take the case of Ian O'Shea, who I'm also fairly certain she killed. It was known around the office that they were an item, which was a convenient excuse as to why her DNA was found at his apartment. She killed him and tried to pin it on Carl Deere—"

"You don't know that for certain."

"Not yet," he admitted. "But look at the facts. She believed O'Shea was Ghost Squad—"

The driver laughed, in bad taste.

"—whereas he was just a decent bloke who happened to have worked undercover on Deere's original case. Ava killed him because she thought he was spying on her, which is why she was so upset when she found out she was wrong."

"It might have been Deere," the driver said, and started the engine so they could turn up the heat inside the car.

"It didn't match his MO," Carter said.

"Neither did bludgeoning Ava or that doctor—Palmer, is it?—but he did."

Carter said nothing for a long moment, while another thought circled his mind. "Perhaps that wasn't Carl either," he murmured.

His companion turned to him in surprise. "Look, I know you're invested in this, and you want to bring her in, but we can't go around pinning other crimes on her tail."

"I'm not suggesting we do," he said. "I'm just wondering whether Naomi Palmer gave Ava some reason to silence her."

"Palmer wasn't involved in any of it," the driver replied. "She couldn't know anything about the Carl Deere case—or about Lipman and Vaughn, for that matter."

"She and Gregory are an item," Carter explained. "He would have discussed things with her, I'm sure. Palmer is an intelligent woman, so it's possible she noticed something we didn't. Her mistake was to confide in the wrong person."

"Conjecture," the driver replied, and yawned hugely. "Sorry, early start this morning. Look, I know Ava changed her surname and it's possible she did that to hide her connection with Daniel Nkosi, but that isn't a crime. There's no evidence connecting her to the deaths of Lipman or Vaughn, and we don't seem to be getting any closer to acquiring any, even after your best efforts."

"There may not be any evidence, but she doesn't have an alibi for either murder,"

Carter said. "We didn't go into this thinking she was guilty; it was supposed to be a simple task to eliminate her from suspicion, after the investigating team discovered her family connection. We didn't expect her to be without an alibi for either one."

Sensing he was winning, Carter pushed on.

"All I need is more time," he said, and gone was the easy-going, crisp-munching bumbler the outside world mistook him to be. "I'm not wrong, ma'am. I promise you, that."

The driver tapped her nails against the steering wheel.

"A suspicion isn't determinative, and, now that Ava's suffering from amnesia, I can't help but wonder whether we've been chasing a wild goose for the past three years," she said. "There are other cases, Carter. Perhaps our resources would be better spent pursuing those avenues."

He shook his head. "Give me another six months—"

"Not a chance."

He swallowed. "All right, then. *Three.* Three more months," he argued. "I think Ava remembers more than she's letting on, and I've enlisted Gregory to help draw her out."

"You told him?"

"Of course not," Carter muttered. "He doesn't know anything about our suspicions, and I don't think he knows anything about her connection to the Nkosi case—why would he? It was before his time, and he has no reason to suspect she's changed her name unless she tells him about it. All the same, it doesn't stop the good doctor being useful to us."

His section manager in Ghost Squad pointed a manicured finger. "Keep it clean, Carter, and make it fast," she said. "The Nkosi case was a stain on the department, and a sensation in the press. Students still talk about it in their Criminology classes, and God knows I still hear about it from the brass, every time one of ours lets the side down. It doesn't help that Lipman and Vaughn were two of the worst examples of policing the Met has ever seen. If we move on Ava Hope, we have to be absolutely certain, because it'll rake the whole case up again and bring the department into disrepute for a second time. It'll be both of our jobs, if we're wrong."

Carter knew it. "There's only one surviving member of the gang believed to have killed Daniel Nkosi, back in '95," he said.

"I know—he's in prison for drugs trafficking."

"Due out on parole next week," Carter said.

She considered the new information. "The other two gang members died in suspected drug overdoses—correct?"

"Yes, and the toxicology reports from both suggest the drugs came from the same batch," he said. "Easy enough for someone to get their hands on some coke, and cut it with something more potent."

"Conjecture again," she said, but it was possible.

Oh yes, it was possible.

"Tell me more about the third," she said.

"Paul Flint," Carter replied. "He was banged up for trafficking a few years ago, but he's still the head of the gang. He has a deputy running his business on the ground but he's out for good behaviour next week, so he'll probably take back the reins, or try to."

"You think Ava plans to kill him, as soon as he's out?"

Carter picked at his teeth. "I think, if she's done for Lipman and Vaughn, and seen off the other two who killed her brother, then there's every chance she'd want to finish what she started."

"At least she can't walk very far, at the moment."

"So she says."

There was a long silence, during which time they stared out of the windshield at the deserted car park but saw only their duty, and the task they were entrusted to do.

"All right," she said eventually. "You've got three months."

"Thank you, ma'am."

CHAPTER 7

Xavier House, 1995

"I'm very sorry, Mr Nkosi, but there's nothing more we can do."

DI Lipman stood with his hands clasped, while DS Vaughn fidgeted beside him and wished for a cigarette or something stronger.

"Your feet are dirty."

He looked across at Irene, who'd lost half her body weight in the weeks since her son had died, and whose waif-like figure was huddled into one of her living room chairs.

"Sorry?"

"Your *feet*," she enunciated, very clearly. "They're spreading muck on my rug."

Vaughn rolled his eyes. "Sorry about that," he forced himself to say.

As if she lived in a palace, he thought, snidely.

Irene continued to stare at the ground, retreating into a silent, private world where she could imagine Daniel was still alive. She could almost hear his voice, deeper than it used to be as a little boy, calling out to her.

Mum! I'm home!

What's for tea?

Tears leaked from her eyes and down her face. Noticing them, Vaughn averted his gaze and reminded himself that there were always casualties in war and in business. He had nothing against her personally—even if she *had* shacked up with an immigrant rather than sticking to one of her own—but neither he nor Lipman could afford to allow the death of one South London kid to interfere with the smooth running of the drugs trade that lined their pockets on a weekly basis.

"As I was saying, Mr Nkosi, unfortunately we haven't been able to apprehend any suspects in your son's murder," Lipman continued. "It's been one of those cases where we have no reliable witnesses and no forensic evidence to point the finger at any one person—"

James held up both hands, which shook slightly as his body craved the next hit of whisky.

As soon as they left, he told himself. *He'd go down to Mr Ali's and pick up another bottle.*

"That doesn't make sense," he said, as calmly as he could for a man who'd lost his only son. "You say you've got no witnesses, but I've heard rumours myself around the estate about who it was! All you have to do is pull your finger out—"

"Now, then, Mr Nkosi, there's no need for any of that," Vaughn said, firmly. "As DI Lipman has already told you, we're doing our best down at The Yard, and we'll carry on investigating until we've followed every avenue. Obviously, we understand this is difficult—"

"Do you?" Irene said softly, and raised watery eyes that saw through to his very soul. "Have you lost a child, sergeant?"

His jaw clenched, but he shook his head.

"Then, you know *nothing* about how we feel," she whispered. "You see tragedy every day, so, maybe all the people who die are just names and numbers to you. To us, they're our children, our sons and daughters, our sisters and brothers. Daniel was everything to us, sergeant. *Everything*. Now, he's nothing but a spirit on the wind."

She went back to staring at the carpet, and James moved to put a hand on her shoulder.

"I don't believe there are no witnesses," he said, after a moment passed. "There was a crowd around him, when you arrived. Didn't one of them see somethin'? They must have done."

Lipman rubbed the side of his nose. "Our officers interviewed everyone who was there that night," he said, evasively. "As you know, with it being winter, it was dark when your son was attacked. Even if anyone had seen something, their testimony would be very unreliable in court, so it's unlikely the Crown Prosecution Service would take the case forward. We have to think of these things, Mr Nkosi."

"But surely you must have found *some* evidence?"

"We are still tracing the source of those drugs."

Irene looked up at that, and then away again.

"We've already told you, they weren't Daniel's," James said. "He wasn't a user, or a dealer. Why don't you re-interview everyone in the building here, and see what they say? I'm tellin' you, I've heard some names bein' mentioned—"

"That's hearsay, Mr Nkosi, and we can't build a case from that, either," Lipman told him. "Now, why not leave it to the professionals, and we'll update you as soon as we can."

"It's already been weeks without any progress."

"Some cases are solved quickly, while others take a bit longer," Vaughn said, in his most condescending tone. "You just wait by the phone, and we'll call you when we have something. Bye, now."

They turned to leave, and almost barrelled into a girl of nine or ten who'd been standing behind them, listening quietly. She wore a pink fluffy onesie and an expression that was far older than her years, leaving both men with the impression that her dark eyes had seen straight through to their rotten cores.

"Mind out the way, love," Vaughn said, and stepped around her to make for the front door and the freedom beyond it.

Lipman followed but, at the last moment, turned back to find the girl still watching him with that unnerving expression in her eye. "Past your bedtime," he muttered, and let the door slam on his way out.

CHAPTER 8

London, Present Day

The Houses of Parliament were resplendent in the early morning sunshine.

It was true that familiarity could sometimes breed contempt, but, as he and Bill crossed the river and looked upon the Palace of Westminster, Alex found himself just as awed by the architecture as he had ever been. Its Gothic Revival design had been conceived by Sir Charles Barry, constructed in 1837 and designated a UNESCO World Heritage Site more than a hundred years later, but some form of palace had stood upon the same foundations since at least the time of Edward the Confessor before falling prey to major fires in the sixteenth and nineteenth centuries. Now, its mellow stonework beckoned them to step inside and retrace the footsteps of kings and rogues, who had, at times, been one and the same.

Parliamentary offices were split across three different sites in Parliament Square, but it happened that Jonathan Smythe, Rt. Honourable Member of Parliament for Greenwich and Woolwich, had been allocated an office within the main palace complex. Alex and Bill therefore joined a long queue and spent forty minutes making their way through stringent security checks before entering the cavernous Hall of Westminster, from which they were directed through a warren of smaller corridors and rooms towards Smythe's office suite. There, they were greeted by a man of around forty with an impressive beard and a nervous demeanour.

"Dr Gregory? Professor Douglas? Thank God, you're here. I'm Henry Gardiner," he said, and shook their hands. "Senior Parliamentary Aide to Mr Smythe."

He led them through an ante room and then, after a brief knock, into Smythe's personal sanctum.

"Mr Smythe? I have Professor Douglas and Doctor Gregory to see you."

Jonathan Smythe was a tall, thin man in his late fifties, whose face bore the ravages of a sleepless night. "Thank you for coming," he said. "I believe you already know Chief Constable Porter?"

They turned to find Porter seated in one of the visitors' chairs—a forcible reminder that MPs tended to have friends in high places.

"We haven't met, but I know you both by reputation, of course," he said.

"Likewise," Alex replied, and Porter's lips twitched.

"Yes, I imagine DCI Hope would have mentioned my name, prior to her injury," he said. "Well, let me be straight with you, Doctor—Professor. I advised Mr Smythe expressly against engaging any so-called criminal profiling experts, because, in my experience, all they do is muddy the waters. When a child's life is at stake, there's nobody better placed to help than the police." He reached for his cup of tea, which rested neatly on a saucer on the table at his elbow.

"That being said, the decision is Mr Smythe's to make," he continued. "He believes your insights might help our investigation and, if that's the case, we certainly won't cut off our nose to spite our face."

It was more than they'd expected to hear from any of the senior personnel at the Met, so Gregory and Douglas took it as a major concession.

"Mr Smythe? Was there anything you wanted to say, before I apprise them of the facts?"

The MP leaned back against his enormous captain's desk, and shook his head. "Go ahead."

Gregory was concerned about the man's colour, which seemed unusually ruddy, but told himself to focus on what Porter was trying to tell them.

"Having gone to bed at the usual time of seven-thirty, Mr Smythe's son, Rory, was found to be missing from his bedroom at approximately eleven-thirty last night, when his mother happened to look in to check on him before going to bed herself," Porter began. "Mrs Smythe made a thorough and immediate search of the house and, when she found no trace of him, she alerted Mr Smythe, who was reading some papers in their bedroom."

Smythe nodded, remembering the look on his wife's face.

Rory's missing, Jon! I can't find him anywhere—

"There were no obvious signs of a break-in," Porter was saying. "Our working theory is that Rory left the house of his own accord, possibly having been lured outside for a pre-planned rendezvous or for some other reason."

Gregory made swift notes on his phone, while Douglas listened.

"Mr Smythe made a search of the area around the house, which is in Greenwich, then returned to call in a Missing Persons report," Porter said. "Officers were dispatched shortly afterwards."

He paused, and Alex took his chance to ask a few pertinent questions.

"Do you have private security, Mr Smythe?"

He nodded.

"Yes, my driver doubles as my bodyguard," he said. "Unfortunately, it was Gordon's evening off, last night."

"We checked him out," Porter said, before Alex could ask. "He has an alibi. Gordon Jenkins attends night school on Thursday evenings at Birkbeck College, which is corroborated by his classmates and tutor, all of whom went for some social drinks at the pub after class and stayed there until at least eleven. There would have been no time for him to leave and return to Mr Smythe's house in Greenwich during such a short window of time, let alone to kidnap Rory."

It didn't preclude his having any involvement, Alex thought, but filed it away for later.

"What about CCTV?" Douglas asked. "Any other security?"

Smythe nodded. "We have cameras at the front and back of the house, and on one of the side elevations, but on the other side I'm afraid the camera is broken, and we haven't got around to replacing it," he said.

"When was it broken?" Alex asked.

"I know what you're thinking, Doctor, but the camera wasn't sabotaged in this case," he said. "We have a basketball hoop fixed to that side of the house, which is occasionally used by my son and his friends, and unfortunately a ball went astray a few weeks ago and smashed into the camera."

"Nonetheless, if someone happened to find out the camera was broken, it would be a convenient entrance and exit point," Gregory remarked. "Is Rory's bedroom on that side of the house?"

Smythe shook his head. "No, but there is a utility room window that's very accessible on the ground floor, as well as several other downstairs sash windows that could be opened, as well as the back door."

"Were any of the windows found ajar?" Alex asked, and Porter shook his head.

"No, none. The CCTV doesn't show anyone leaving or entering the house from the front either. As Mr Smythe says, the back door could have been a possibility, but it was locked from the inside—the keys were still inside the lock."

"And neither you, nor Mrs Smythe, locked the door after the relevant time?"

Smythe shook his head. "My wife tends to do that, and she did indeed check the back door, but found it was already locked."

"Does Rory have a set of house keys, or are there any missing?"

Smythe shook his head, again. "No, we tend to accompany him everywhere—for *safety*," he said, voice trembling on the last, fateful word. "He never needed his own house keys, as he's still only eight and we drive everywhere. As for any other keys being missing, we found all of them present and accounted for."

"I understand there was a ransom note?" Douglas prompted.

Smythe nodded, and moved around his desk to bring up the e-mail.

"Here," he said, finding the words blurring in front of his eyes. "You'd better read it, yourselves."

"Thank you," Gregory murmured, and put a hand on the man's arm. "Why not have a seat, Mr Smythe?"

It was on the tip of his tongue to reject the advice, and put on the strong front that had served him so well during his political career, but he could see the sense in it.

"Yes…all right."

He took the chair beside Porter, and they waited while Gregory and Douglas read through the ransom e-mail. It said:

Missing your son, Mr Smythe? He means everything to you, doesn't he?

If that's the case, you won't mind paying for him.

We want a hundred thousand in online bitcoin, or little Rory won't ever be coming home.

The note went on to give the transfer details, but no timescale for payment. It also stipulated that, if they went to the press, they'd never see Rory again.

Alex turned to Porter.

"Do you have people trying to trace the e-mail?"

"Of course—the bitcoin wallet, too," came the reply. "But this is Dark Web stuff, and virtually impossible for an overstretched digital forensics team to handle. We've called in GCHQ to lend a hand, since the matter could concern national security—especially given Mr Smythe's position on the Home Affairs Select Committee."

Alex noted the time of the e-mail, which had been sent on the dot of midnight the previous evening.

"It's unusual that no deadline for payment has been imposed," he said. "Usually, in cases such as these, I'd expect to see one, which makes sense if money is the main objective."

"It could be political," Douglas pointed out. "Beyond the fact you're obviously a known person, Mr Smythe, and occupy a senior position in government, it does beg the question of why you were targeted. Have you been outspoken about any particular issues, lately?"

"You're saying it could be some extremist group?"

Douglas nodded. "It's possible," he said. "Perhaps a smaller one, with an axe to grind against one of your policies, with a need for finance."

"I've had some trouble with local climate campaign groups," Smythe said. "They wanted me to push for a pedestrian zone in Greenwich and Woolwich that simply wasn't feasible, given the road network. They weren't happy."

"We can look into that, if you have the details?" Porter said.

Smythe nodded. "I'll ask Henry to forward them to you."

But every man in the room knew that kind of legwork would take some time, which was a commodity in short supply.

Douglas scratched his chin, and considered the mind of an eight-year-old boy. "If we assume your theory is correct, and Rory left home of his own accord to meet a person or persons unknown, there must have been sufficient incentive," he said. "What kind of things does Rory like?"

Smythe thought of his son, and of the times he'd barked at him to keep the volume down or go and play in his bedroom, and vowed that he'd never do either of those things again. If—*when*—Rory came home, things would be different. "I—ah—I suppose he's just like every other boy his age," he replied. "He likes to play on his Nintendo, when he's allowed some screen time. He likes going to the park, and the funfair. He likes sugar, and foods that are mostly beige in colour. He likes to read…he's a voracious reader, in fact. He can tell you all about the solar system, about prehistoric times, and a good chunk about the Pharaohs, too."

"He sounds like a smart kid," Alex said.

Smythe nodded, but couldn't find the words to reply.

"With your permission, I think it might be useful for us to have a look around Rory's bedroom, and the house in general, to get a lay of the land," Douglas said.

"My team has already done a thorough sweep," Porter said. "They worked through the night."

"I'm sure they've done a stellar job," Alex said. "If the forensic work is already complete, I presume there's no objection to us having a look around?"

Porter's jaw clenched.

"It's settled, then," Smythe said. "I'll tell my wife to expect you."

CHAPTER 9

The Smythe family lived in an elegant, double-fronted Victorian villa in the heart of maritime Greenwich, built of faded red bricks partially covered in trailing ivy. It was picture perfect, Alex thought, and conveyed the impression that everything and everyone who dwelled inside it must be perfect, too. To a certain kind of troubled mind who coveted such things, it presented a temptation to despoil all that lay within its fine walls. With these troubling thoughts swirling, he and Bill pressed the intercom button beside a set of tall iron driveway gates and considered their surroundings while they awaited a reply.

"It's unlikely Rory left the house via this route," Alex remarked. "That CCTV camera would definitely have picked him up, and the gates lead directly onto a fairly busy road, where he could have been seen by a passer-by, or by any of the other cameras on the road or the shops."

"Yes," Bill agreed. "If someone lured him out, they would want to avoid attracting any undue attention, so that wouldn't be ideal."

Just then, a disembodied voice crackled over the intercom. They gave their names, looked into the tiny camera so their faces could be seen, and the gates opened. They proceeded to crunch their way over a short gravel driveway towards a glossy black front door, which was opened by a woman of around thirty.

"Mrs Smythe?"

"No, I'm Stefanie, Mrs Smythe's housekeeper," she said. "You must be Professor Douglas and Dr Gregory. Please come in."

They wiped their feet on the mat and stepped into a shining hallway.

"If you'll follow me," she said. "Mrs Smythe is in the kitchen."

They moved into a large, airy room at the back of the house, which boasted an orangery extension and the most enormous Aga cooker they'd ever seen.

"Hello."

The word was spoken so softly, they almost missed it.

Anita Smythe was seated at one of the kitchen stools, her hands wrapped around a cup of coffee that appeared to be untouched.

"This is Doctor Gregory and Professor Douglas," Stefanie said. "Would you like me to stay, Mrs Smythe?"

Anita Smythe looked between them with a listless expression that marred an otherwise beautiful face.

"It's all right, Stefanie, you can leave us to it. Thank you for coming," she tagged on, once the housekeeper departed. "Would you like some tea or coffee?"

Usually, they would have declined the offer, preferring instead to move straight to the business of fact-finding. However, Anita's pupils were dilated, and there was a tremor to her hands which told them clearly that she needed careful treatment. Sometimes, the distraction of performing ordinary tasks could be beneficial.

"Coffee would be very kind, thank you, Mrs Smythe," Bill said. "We can help?"

"No, it'll give me something to do," she said, and wandered across to an integrated 'bean-to-cup' coffee machine, which she set to percolate. "Jon rang ahead and told me that you want to have a look at Rory's bedroom."

She spoke the words with rigid control, but tears were very close to the surface.

"If that would be okay with you," Alex said.

Anita nodded, and sloshed milk into two cups, which she set in front of them.

"Look wherever you want," she said. "I don't care *what* you do, so long as you help to bring him back. Just—just bring him *home*…"

She broke down, leaning heavily on the counter while she covered her eyes. Bill was closest to her, and moved swiftly to put a supportive arm around her shoulders.

"Come and sit down, Mrs Smythe," he said. "You've had a terrible shock."

He walked her across to a snug area beside the kitchen, where a couple of comfortable sofas had been arranged around a coffee table.

"Here we are," he said, lowering her onto one of them.

Alex followed with a box of tissues he'd taken from the counter, along with a small tin marked 'biscuits' which he'd found beside the kettle. It was a good idea to keep blood sugar levels up, and a digestive was never a bad idea at the best of times.

"Jon should be here, at home," she mumbled. "But he wanted to go into the office to give himself something to do, I think. He can't sit still; he says he feels impotent."

It was the same word Gregory had used to describe himself only a few hours before, when thinking of Naomi's condition. It was a terrible purgatory to live in, each day, and so much worse when a child was involved.

"Jon's from that sort of background, you see," Anita continued. "Boarding school from the age of five, and nobody to talk to, really. He still finds it hard to express his feelings."

"Have you been together a long time?" Douglas asked her, in a deliberate attempt to guide her mind to think of ordinary things rather than catastrophic ones.

"Twelve years," she said. "Jon was married to his first wife, Sally, for seven years and they had Theo."

"Theo?"

"That's Rory's half-brother. He's nine years older, and lives with his mother most of the time, except during the holidays when we alternate. He's with us for the Christmas break, although with everything that's been going on...."

"Do the boys get along?" Alex asked.

"It can be difficult, in some families," she said. "But, honestly, Theo has been a wonderful big brother to Rory, right from the very beginning. He's a teenager, so he has his moments, but when it comes to their relationship, we've never had any cause for concern. He was beside himself, when he heard what had happened, and he was here in the house with us the whole time." Her eyes glazed over again. "Why would anyone do this?" she whispered.

"That's what we're going to find out," Douglas assured her.

A short while later, and with Anita's permission, they began to search the house. What they searched for, they didn't know, but they needed to gain an insight into the personality of the missing boy in order to see whatever his kidnapper might have seen, and exploited to their advantage. There were occasional, sensational cases where a charismatic serial killer managed to disarm an unsuspecting victim, and Gregory and Douglas had treated plenty of them. But, in the main, successful crimes relied on the same principles as any other endeavour: namely, good planning and preparation, a bit of hard work and a lot of determination. People tended to follow a similar routine in their daily lives, and this was especially the case for the Smythe family, whose children attended school at set times and were ferried back and forth by chauffeured car at the same time each morning and evening. With some reconnaissance work, it would have been easy to note the housekeeper's regular hours or days off, alongside Smythe's driver and bodyguard. In this case, Stefanie worked regular nine-to-five hours three days per week, and therefore had not been in the house during the time Rory was taken. As for the driver, they already knew it had been his day off.

They moved through the downstairs rooms, noting the display of framed family photographs, many of which featured a smiling, curly-haired Rory at varying stages of development.

"He's very loved," Alex said, and picked up one of the photographs which showed Jonathan and Anita Smythe with baby Rory in her arms, and an older boy sitting beside them. Seeing it triggered a memory, and an image flashed into Alex's head of a time before his father left them and his mother became severely unwell. He and his brother had been playing on the lawn at their home in Richmond. Heavily pregnant with their sister, his mother had come outside with a picnic basket and blanket, and they'd eaten chicken legs and cocktail sausages, cheese and crackers while the birds sang around their heads. It was a memory he'd clung to for many years, during the hardest, darkest times, but he knew that house and the family who'd dwelled in it had been built upon a foundation of sand.

He put the photograph back, and stepped away.

"Let's try upstairs," he said.

Rory's room had been painted sky blue, except for the ceiling, which had been painted a deep shade of navy.

"Unusual scheme," Bill remarked.

Alex didn't reply, but looked around the room, his eyes tracing over the bed with its blue striped cover and stack of books piled beside it, then on to the overflowing bookcase filled with stories and encyclopaedias, and finally at a child's desk laden with what he would describe as 'boy paraphernalia'. The room had been dusted for prints by the police and still bore the musty scent of it, as well as a fine layer that had settled on much of the furniture. A poster of the planetary system had been tacked to one wall, and a small projector in the shape of the moon took pride of place on the boy's bedside table.

"I think we've found the reason for the dark ceiling," he said, and moved across to switch it on.

Immediately, planets began to swirl overhead, and the two men watched them for a moment or two, feeling like boys again.

"Greenwich Observatory's just around the corner from here," Bill said, when Alex turned the machine off again. "If Rory has an affinity with the stars, he's in the right place for it."

Alex moved to each of the three windows in the room and stopped at the third, where a telescope had been set up.

He leaned down to peer through it.

"You can see the observatory," he confirmed. "I think we've found at least one thing Rory Smythe loved."

"Who're you?"

Both men turned to find a boy of seventeen standing in the doorway, looking at them with open suspicion. He wore baggy jeans, overlong hair, and a t-shirt emblazoned with the Rolling Stones on the front of it.

"I'm going to call Anita," Theo said, and turned as if to run.

"Hold it!" Alex said. "I'm Doctor Gregory, this is Professor Douglas. We're here to help find your brother."

"What are a couple of doctors gonna do to find Rory?"

It was a fair question.

"Whatever we can," Bill replied, with a smile. "We work with the police to create criminal profiles. You must be Theo?"

The boy nodded. "Yeah. I don't know if you're supposed to be in here—"

"It's alright, we've had permission from the police, and from Anita."

Theo looked around his brother's bedroom. "He's only little," he said, and they heard the emotion in his voice. "Why d'you think they took him, and not me?"

"As you said, because he's only little," Alex replied.

Theo nodded, and his chin quivered. "D' you think they did it because of my dad's job?"

"Possibly. What do you think?" Bill asked.

"Me? I dunno…I guess, I think, someone wants my dad to do something he doesn't wanna do? Or, like, pay them some money, or something like that? Why doesn't he just do it, then Rory can come home?"

"Your father is restrained by his government role—he can't be at the mercy of terrorists or blackmailers."

Theo shrugged his skinny shoulders. "Well, I guess I know what would happen to me, if I'd been the one who was taken," he said, with irrefutable logic.

"Kidnapping cases are handled extremely carefully," Bill assured him. "Everybody is working around the clock, doing all they can."

Theo didn't seem overly convinced.

"Did you hear anything, last night?" Alex asked.

"No, nothing until Anita came running into my room asking if I'd seen him," he said.

"What time was that—do you remember?"

Theo shrugged again. "Maybe half past eleven? I dunno. I told the police everything I could remember, anyway."

He looked between them, then at the bed where his brother usually slept.

"Look, he's gonna come home, isn't he? I mean…what if you can't find him? What happens then?"

"Let's not think about that," Bill said.

Theo nodded, and his surly, teenage face appeared years younger as he appealed to them both.

"Y' know, back when my dad and Anita said they were having a baby…I guess I was angry because I thought they were replacing me. I didn't think I'd be able to like Rory, but I was wrong about that. He's easy to love."

He reddened a bit, obviously embarrassed by his own admission.

Bill put a hand on the boy's shoulder.

"We'll do everything we can to help. In the meantime, your stepmother could use some company, don't you think? Why don't you sit with her and watch a movie, to take your mind off things for a little while?"

"Yeah, I guess I could."

With that, he slunk out of the room and, a moment later, they heard his clattering footsteps descend the staircase.

"Seems a nice kid," Bill remarked, once he was out of earshot.

Alex nodded. "Blended families aren't always so easy to navigate," he said. "We need to ask about his mother—Smythe's first wife."

Bill agreed. "I think we should take a look at the school, and speak to some of his friends and their families. Anita has given us a list of the ones who've been to the house, here, and would know its layout."

"The school is closed for the holidays," Alex pointed out. "But that doesn't mean there isn't a connection. We should speak to Porter about tracking down the people on that list, and add some of Anita's friends, and Smythe's friends, too. There's a pool of potential suspects, but they all had to have known Rory and would have been in a position to manipulate him."

The pool seemed to be getting bigger, and the urgency of the situation was not lost on either of them.

"Come on," Bill said. "There's no time to waste."

CHAPTER 10

South London, 1995

DI Lipman and DS Vaughn parked their unmarked car in the forecourt of an old scrap yard, and turned off the headlights. The interior carried the heady scent of fast food, since they'd decided to make a short detour for a couple of Big Macs on their way to the meeting.

"He's always late, anyway," Lipman said, and took a healthy bite.

Vaughn mumbled something, and a bit of half-chewed bread fell from his mouth.

"Slob," Lipman laughed.

"Oh, bugger, he's early for once," Vaughn said, and swiped the back of his hand over his oily chin. "Look."

Lipman peered through the windscreen and watched a souped-up Volkswagen Golf turn into the forecourt. There appeared to be three people inside the car, all of whom they recognised.

He turned on the ignition, and flashed his lights twice.

There came a single flash in return.

"All right, here we go," he said, and, with some regret, wrapped his burger up to finish later.

The two men stepped out of the car, both carrying non-police-issued firearms, in case of emergency. They made their way towards the other car and, as they did, its doors opened and three young men stepped out, each dressed in tracksuits and baseball caps. There was a clear leader amongst them, and he stood out not only because of how he carried himself, but because of the angry-looking scar which ran from the top of one cheek to the edge of his mouth. It had been popular amongst certain corners of the criminal fraternity to gift their enemies a 'Chelsea Smile', which meant slashing a knife from both edges of the mouth to inflict extreme pain and a permanent scar as a warning to others.

In the case of Paul Flint, they'd only managed to complete half a smile, before he'd disarmed his attacker and stuck the knife in his gullet.

"Y'all right, Paul?" Lipman said, in his affable Liverpudlian twang.

Flint rubbed the excess cocaine from his nose, and folded his arms across his chest. "Yer, not bad," came the reply.

"Well, that's good, because—*confidentially*—we heard you'd got into a bit o' bother over at Xavier House the other week," Vaughn said.

Paul looked at the two men flanking him on either side. "We definitely didn't 'ave any *bother*, did we, lads?"

They grinned, and shook their heads.

"Nope, must be another case of mistaken identity, officers. You know us white boys all look alike."

They all laughed at that.

"Listen, just keep a low profile for a while," Lipman told them, after they'd lit up a few cigarettes and chewed the fat. "We've smoothed it over for now, but try to keep your noses clean, for all our sakes. We don't want anyone looking too hard at our little enterprise, do we?"

Paul took a drag of his cigarette, and blew a long trail of smoke into the air. "Well, it wouldn't look too good for you, would it, Detective Inspector?"

Lipman stared at him through the semi-darkness and then, very slowly, very deliberately, crushed his cigarette beneath the heel of his shoe. "Now, listen to me," he growled. "This cuts both ways. You might think you're King Dick now, but, without us, your whole house would fall down—*understand*? We're your Fairy Godmother, you little prick, so just remember that."

There was a tense silence, and then, suddenly, Paul grinned. "Alright, Grandpa, keep your hair on," he said, and they all laughed again—even Lipman.

"There were witnesses at Xavier House," Vaughn said. "They might come forward, and we could do without the hassle."

That wiped the smile from Paul's face. "What witnesses?" he said. "There was one old bloke who shouted down at us, but he couldn't have seen anythin' at that time of night."

"Well, he did, and he said one of the perps had a scar," Lipman told him.

Paul scratched the jagged line on the side of his face.

"Coincidence," he said. "I ain't the only bloke in London to have a scar."

"Yeah, well, I took precautions, just in case," Vaughn said. "Planted a bag of hash on the kid, to make him look like a dealer. Juries and *Daily Mail* readers don't have a lot of sympathy for drug dealers."

"That 'urts me," Paul said, and put a hand to his heart.

"All right, Funny Man, that's enough of the small talk," Lipman said, and held out the palm of his hand. "Hand over what's owed."

Flint nudged the young man to his left, who retrieved an envelope from inside his hoodie.

Lipman took it, took a quick look inside, and nodded. "Pleasure doin' business with you," he said.

"Wait a minute," Vaughn said, as they were about to disband. "Aren't you forgettin' our bonus?"

Paul thought, idly, that he looked forward to a day when he could put them both in the ground. However, until that happy day, he took out a couple of bags of coke and chucked them over.

"Careful," he said. "It's addictive, you know."

On which note, they laughed again, and made their farewells.

As Lipman and Vaughn polished off the rest of their burgers, James Nkosi made his fourth journey in as many days to Mr Ali's Corner Shop for bread and milk, which was the excuse he gave to his wife and daughter.

In truth, he needed a drink, and he needed it badly.

Thoughts of Daniel swirled his mind every waking minute, and long after he went to sleep. He couldn't escape his son's sweet face and a part of him didn't want to. He never wanted to forget how Daniel looked, nor the sound of his voice, so he accepted the haunting without complaint. It robbed him of sleep and of sanity, but a hit of whisky or vodka often took the edge off. A few more rounds, and he became happily drunk, stupefied in an imaginary place where Daniel and he could talk and laugh together, and he could pretend his son was still alive.

James pushed open the jingling door to their local shop.

"Mr Nkosi. Back so soon?"

"Ah—yes, yes, we needed—we need a few things."

James made a token grab for some milk and bread and then headed to the counter.

"Um, just these," he said, and Mr Ali's shoulders relaxed briefly.

"That'll be—"

"Oh, and I'll have a bottle of the Glenfiddich, since I'm here."

Ali looked at him closely. He wasn't drunk, and he was certainly over the age of eighteen, but...

"Are you sure?" he found himself asking.

James stared at him. "W-what?"

"I asked if you're sure," Ali said, quietly. "It's the fourth bottle this week, Mr Nkosi."

Anger fought with embarrassment, and won. "I come here to shop," he snapped. "I can take my business elsewhere—"

Ali looked away, and thought of the polite boy who'd never again come through his door. "My wife and I were so sorry...about what happened to Daniel," he said. "No parent should suffer as you've suffered."

James could only nod, as his hands gripped the counter.

"Have the police made any progress?" Ali wanted to know. He'd been expecting one of them to come and question him but, as yet, no constable had called.

James ran a hand over his eyes. "They've done nothin'," he muttered. "Daniel—he doesn't matter to them."

"Because of the colour of his skin?" Ali said.

James lifted a shoulder. "Could be," he replied. "He's mixed race, so maybe that's some of it. The police don't treat us with respect. Nobody calls to ask if we're okay, or to give us any update. We're always the ones chasin' them. They say they found drugs on 'im but, you know my Daniel—"

"He wasn't one of them," Ali agreed, having seen enough of the local kids to know which ones were running for the gangs, and which ones weren't.

"Still, they found the drugs."

"Maybe one of the ones who attacked him dropped something?" Ali suggested.

James nodded, but his eyes strayed to the whisky again. "Please—" he said.

Ali sighed, but turned and reached for a bottle. He didn't like it, but then, he'd never lost his only son. Krishnan was at university in Leeds studying dentistry, with his whole life ahead of him, not dead and buried at the hands of local thugs.

Who was he to judge?

"Give my best wishes to your wife and daughter, Mr Nkosi."

"Thank you."

James snatched up the bag, and couldn't make it beyond the end of the street before he had to stop and take a long sip of the warming liquid, which spread through his belly and veins like fire. When he let himself back into the flat ten minutes later, there was no sign of Irene, who'd gone to bed, but Ava waited for him in the living room.

"Daddy?"

His hand gripped the plastic bag, and he was irritated by the interruption. "I—yes? What is it?"

Ava looked down at her feet, scared to say anything.

James shook himself, and set the bag down on the dining table, moving across the room to lift her up into his arms. "Sorry, my princess," he muttered. "I didn't mean to shout. What were you goin' to ask me?"

"I'm hungry," she said. "Mum forgot to make any dinner."

He closed his eyes, which had filled with tears, and set her back on her feet. "Oh dear," he said. "You know, your mum hasn't been very well since—since—"

"Daniel went with the angels."

"That's right." He led her into the kitchen, and propped her up onto the counter while he set about making a fat omelette with the eggs and cheese he found in the fridge.

They'd do better tomorrow, he told himself. *For Ava's sake.*

"All right, Princess," he said, a few minutes later. "Here you go."

They sat at the dining table awhile, and he tried to listen to her chatter about school, but the plastic carrier bag taunted him, and he found himself wishing she would eat faster and go to bed so that he could be alone with his whisky and his memories.

CHAPTER 11

London, Present Day

Ava stared at the glass of apple juice she held in one hand, then at the small collection of white pills in the other.

"Are you all right?"

She looked across at Alex, and nodded. "Yes, sorry, I was just daydreaming."

She knocked back the medication, thanked the nurse who hovered at her side, and then leaned back against the chair she occupied in the residents' lounge. The room was quiet at that time of day, and she and Alex had the place to themselves.

"How are you feeling?"

She looked at the collection of posters adorning the walls, alongside a line of 'thank you' cards which had been strung like bunting on a piece of string hanging from one corner of the room to the other.

"Things keep coming in snapshots," she said. "For instance, when I was drinking my apple juice just now, I had a clear vision of the same-coloured liquid in a whisky glass—you know, one of the old-fashioned, cut-glass tumblers?"

"That's interesting," he said. "Where was the glass?"

"What do you mean?"

He made a rolling gesture with his hand. "I mean, was it on a table, in somebody's hand, or elsewhere?"

"Oh, I see…um, it was on a table, I think," she said, and closed her eyes, trying to recall the image. "Yes! It was. I think it might have been quite an old table, one of the Formica ones from the seventies, with a laminated top. You know the kind?"

"Yes, I know the kind you mean. Do you remember anything else about the surroundings, or who the glass belonged to?"

"I can see wallpaper in the background," she said slowly. "It has a kind of cream, floral pattern on it."

"Seventies as well, do you think?"

"Actually, it feels more like the nineties," she replied. "I don't know why."

"You do know why, but we'll get to that," he said, with a smile.

"Do you think it was whisky in the glass?"

She nodded.

"Do you like whisky?"

Her nose wrinkled. "I can't *stand* the stuff," she said, vehemently.

Too vehemently? he wondered.

"Do you know anybody who does like whisky?"

"My dad," she said, without thinking.

This was an interesting development, he thought, since she'd never mentioned her father before, and they'd never seen him around the hospital.

"Perhaps we can ask him about it?"

"I don't think so."

"Why not?"

"I think," she said, speaking very softly. "I think he might be dead." She looked up at him with an anguished expression. "I don't know if that's true, or if I'm thinking of one of my old cases," she said.

"We could ask your mum," he suggested.

Ava nodded, and became restless. "I can't remember what he looks like," she said. "Why do I think he's dead, but can't even remember his face?"

"It's sad news, if you're right about it," he replied, and leaned forward to give her hand a friendly squeeze in support. "But memories don't always come back in a linear, organised way. They come back in pieces or fragments sometimes. Try not to worry about it and just let them come. We can organise them later."

She gnawed on her lip, but nodded.

"Think about that wallpaper again," he said, and she frowned.

"Why?"

"Humour me," he said. "That is, if you're willing to remember?"

She closed her eyes, finding it was easier to recall the image of cream-coloured flowers without any distractions.

"What kind of flowers are on the paper?"

"Roses," she replied. "Tiny cream roses."

"Does the wallpaper go all around the room, or just part of it?"

"All around," she replied. "It stops at the kitchen door."

"What about the floor?" he asked her. "Is it carpet, wood, or tile?"

"It's laminate wood," she replied. "My dad fitted it, recently."

Recently? he thought.

"Did he? What about the furniture? Did he make any of it?"

"No, the sofa was a gift," she replied. "From the church."

"That's very kind," Gregory replied. "Do you go to church?"

"No," she said, flatly. "Not since I was a child."

Something to explore later, he thought.

"What about the kitchen, Ava? What does it look like?"

"It's small and white, with grey counters," she replied. "Mum keeps herbs in pots on the window ledge, so it always smells of basil or mint."

"Can you see anything from the window in the kitchen, Ava?"

Her eyebrows drew together in another frown. "The rest of the estate," she said. "There's a quad in the middle, covered in grass, but we're quite high up so you can only see a bit of it."

"Can you hear anything?"

"I can hear the radio playing in my bedroom."

"Which song?"

"*Angels* by Robbie Williams," she replied, and began to hum the tune.

"What does your bedroom look like?"

She was silent for a long moment, and then opened her eyes. "I can't see it," she replied. "I can hear the music, but I can't see it."

"Never mind," he said. "You've done really well, today, but you'll be feeling tired now."

He was right, for she felt as though she'd just completed a marathon.

"I have to get going, anyway," Alex said.

"To see Naomi?"

"Yes, but I've also got some work to do."

"I thought you said you'd taken a break away from Southmoor?"

"Well remembered," he said. "But this isn't Southmoor work. Bill and I were offered a profiling case, last night."

"Let me know if you need any help," she said. "My memory might resemble a sieve, but I'm told I used to be quite good at investigating things. Besides, you're doing so much to help me, it would be nice to reciprocate in some way."

"The best way you can reciprocate is by continuing to get better," he said. "But I'll keep the offer in mind. Look after yourself, Ava."

"Alex?"

He stopped at the door, and looked back.

"Say 'hello' to Naomi, from me."

"I will."

After he left, she stood up, and made her way back to the safety of her hospital bed.

CHAPTER 12

When Alex reached Naomi's room, he found she was not alone.

A woman in her late sixties was seated beside her, and reminded him very much of the actress Meryl Streep, with her soft blonde hair and elegant features. Elizabeth Palmer looked nothing like her daughter, whom she'd adopted as a baby, but their bond was inseparable.

"Hello, Elizabeth," he said.

She looked across as he entered. "Hello, Alex," she said, in the same crisp, East Coast accent she'd passed on to Naomi.

"I thought you were flying back to New York, this week?" he said, and drew up a chair on the opposite side of the bed.

"Geoff has flown back," she said, referring to her husband. "He has to see to some things back home, but, when it came to it...I just couldn't leave her."

Alex looked at Naomi, who slept beside them, and nodded. "I understand."

They fell into a comfortable silence for a while, before Elizabeth spoke again.

"The doctors say she demonstrated some brain activity, this morning. She opened her eyes several times, too."

Alex came to attention. "That's *wonderful*," he said, and felt terrible that he hadn't been there. "What are the next steps?"

Elizabeth avoided his eyes. "There aren't any, according to the doctors here, except to let time do its work," she said. "But I might as well tell you, Alex, that we don't think they're doing enough to help her. We—her father and I, that is—we feel Naomi would be better off at home, in New York. We can give her the finest medical care, there."

Alex told himself to remain calm, and his voice was rigidly so when he replied. "The flight alone would be detrimental," he said. "Think of the air pressure at altitude, and the possible impact on her brain and other vital organs."

Elizabeth's mouth firmed into a stubborn line. "If the doctors say it's possible, then it's possible."

"I'm sure anything is possible," he replied. "Whether it's *advisable* is another matter entirely."

"I know you care about Naomi," Elizabeth said, in a stern voice. "But we are her parents. You must allow us to know what's best for her."

"With the greatest of respect, I think it's for Naomi's medical team to know what's best for her."

Elizabeth wanted to argue, but found that she couldn't. "Then we'll ask them."

Gregory nodded, and went off in search of a consultant with a couple of minutes to spare—which was no easy task, in a busy hospital, but eventually he found one of the neurologists managing Naomi's case and the man agreed to speak with them.

"Mrs Palmer? I'm John Brosnan, one of the consultant neurologists here," he said, as he swept into the room. "I understand you'd like some advice."

Elizabeth nodded. "Yes, thank you, Doctor. As you know, Naomi's American, and we live in New York," she said. "I understand that, in the first few weeks after her injury, it made sense not to move her. But now, her father and I really feel it's time to take her home and oversee her care from there."

Brosnan listened attentively, while Gregory stood back and told himself he would cope with whatever outcome, even if it meant emigrating to New York.

"I understand how you feel, Mrs Palmer," the consultant said, in a tone that was both firm and gentle at the same time. "However, I must strongly advise against moving Naomi. Her condition, although stable, is still very fragile and we shouldn't expose her to unnecessary risk."

Elizabeth heard the sense in what he said, and saw the kindness reflected in his eyes and that of the man standing just beyond his shoulder, and started to cry.

"I'm—I'm sorry," she said. "I'm just so desperate to help her. I thought—we thought—

if we could only get her home, it would make a—a difference—"

Brosnan murmured some words of comfort, then excused himself and moved on to the next urgent case. Gregory stepped forward and took Elizabeth's hand between his own.

"You love her," he said, deeply. "Of course, you want to do all you can for her."

Elizabeth nodded, helplessly.

"I feel the same way," he said. "Unfortunately, neither of us can fix her. We have to wait, and hope that her brain can fix itself, given enough time."

She looked into his steady green eyes and wanted, desperately, to believe that time healed all wounds. Unfortunately, having lived more of life than he had, she'd come to learn that it wasn't always the case.

"Alex," she said. "There may come a time when you have to prepare yourself, as I will have to. Nobody would blame you, if you chose to step back sooner rather than later."

He knew that she meant well, but the words were anathema to him.

"I have no intention of stepping back," he said. "For as long as I'm welcome here, I'll sit beside her and hold her hand, talk to her, and remind her of all the things she has to look forward to."

Elizabeth managed a smile. "You must really love my daughter," she said.

"Yes," he said simply.

"She's lucky, then."

Alex had agreed to meet Bill at Scotland Yard after his pitstop at the hospital, in time for a two o'clock police briefing of the taskforce dedicated to finding Rory Smythe—aptly named, 'OPERATION GREENWICH'. Sure enough, when he stepped through the automatic doors and into the modern glass atrium that formed the apex of New Scotland Yard, he found his friend waiting for him.

"Thought you'd been held up," Bill said, coming to his feet.

"I was," he replied, thinking of the extra time he'd spent talking with Naomi's mother. "I ran across Lambeth Bridge."

Having been pre-approved for entry, the two men procured some visitors' badges and were directed to one of the upper floors, where the Major Crimes division was housed. However, instead of veering towards Carter's section, they made their way towards Chief Constable Porter's office on the far side of the open plan office, passing several other teams within the Major Crimes division as they went. It was sobering to think of the volume of cases that should require so many teams, but then, London was a capital city with a dense population, so it was perhaps surprising there wasn't more in the way of violent crime, as in other cities around the world.

As they reached Porter's office, the door opened.

"Ah, Doctor Gregory, Professor Douglas," he said. "You're just in time—the briefing is in the conference room, this way."

He led them along a corridor lined with opaque glass meeting rooms.

"How was your visit to Greenwich, this morning?" he threw back over his shoulder.

"Instructive," Alex replied.

Porter stopped, and turned. "How so?"

"Well, for one thing, we know much more about the missing boy than we did," Alex replied. "We've built up a picture of his habits and interests, which will be useful when paired with the statements from the family's wider circle. Some of them may have been better placed than others to command a position of trust in his life, and to use his own interests to lure him out of the house."

Porter nodded. "What do you make of the set-up?" he asked. "It seems to me, the only obvious exit point is the back door, which leads directly out of the house, on the elevation not presently covered by CCTV, and also gives access to the garden side gate which can be opened with a code, which we must presume Rory knew."

"Except, the door was locked from the inside," Bill pointed out. "Anita Smythe is adamant she found it that way, when she did her usual checks of the house."

"The dog flap," Gregory said, suddenly.

"What?" Porter said.

"The family must have had a dog, at one stage or another, because there's a large plastic dog flap fitted to the back door. It's small, but large enough for a boy of eight to shimmy through. That way, he wouldn't need a key, and it would explain why the door was still locked from the inside."

Porter was frustrated that his own team hadn't thought to mention it. He turned and continued striding towards the conference room.

"What we really need is to speak to the family's wider circle—friends, school parents and teachers—" Alex continued.

"Already booked in," Porter said. "My team contacted all the names given to us, and a few more besides. Most of them are coming in for scheduled interviews directly after the briefing this afternoon, and those who can't come in will be visited at home or over the telephone."

They could only be impressed by the hustle.

"Would you have any objection to us observing the interviews?" Gregory asked him.

Porter decided there was no harm in it. "You can observe, but not participate," he said. "If you feel there are any specific questions or lines of questioning that should be covered, let me know."

"Thank you," Bill replied, and realised he was coming to like the surly man with the crop of salt-and-pepper hair and the weight of The Yard on his shoulders.

Porter stopped outside one of the larger conference rooms. "Before we go inside, I need to tell you something else," he said, and looked slightly uncomfortable. "Some of the team here… well, they blame you for DCI Hope's condition. They may not work in the same team as Ava, but the staff in Major Crimes all know one another and socialise, you know how it is. Every officer knows the job carries some risk, especially in circumstances where a manhunt was underway. But—"

"It's human nature," Alex murmured.

"Exactly, and we take the good with the bad."

With that, he pushed open the door and led them inside the bull pen.

CHAPTER 13

London, 1996

James and Irene Nkosi caught the Number 68 bus from Denmark Hill, where Irene had attended an appointment with a grief therapist at the Maudsley Hospital, and made their way north, through Camberwell and along the Walworth Road towards Elephant and Castle. There, they alighted the bus and walked a short distance to the offices of Dryden & Khan Solicitors, who, the advert informed them, were local experts in *all* areas of civil and criminal law. Not being lawyers themselves, and requiring a firm of solicitors that would accept their case on a 'no win, no fee' basis, neither James nor Irene questioned the assertion.

Consequently, they found themselves seated inside a tiny waiting room without natural light or ventilation, which carried a strong chemical scent of floor cleaner. The walls, which were an industrial beige but might once have been painted white, were papered in printed testimonials from past clients, all of whom had rated the firm 'five stars'. In the corner of the room was an oppressively large artificial bamboo plant that towered over a dripping water cooler, which was out of service.

James held a brown envelope in his hands, which he turned over and over, while his knee bobbed up and down in restless anxiety. Irene sat beside him, her thin body huddled into the chair, hair dishevelled from hours of running her fingers through its length.

"Mr and Mrs Nkosi? You can go in, now; Mr Dryden is ready for you."

The receptionist went back to playing solitaire on an ancient desktop computer, and they rose from their chairs to knock on a door bearing Dryden's name.

"Come in!"

They entered a small but meticulously organised space, which even boasted a window. The desk was workmanlike rather than distinguished, and the man seated behind it was diminutive rather than statesmanlike, but there were law degrees and practising certificates framed on the wall behind him, which put them at ease.

"Mr and Mrs Nkosi, I take it? Alfie Dryden, pleased to meet you."

They shook hands, and he invited them to have a seat.

"I understand you have a legal matter you'd like to discuss with me?"

James looked across at Irene, who gave a brief nod.

"It's about—" He cleared his throat. "About our son, Daniel."

"Go on," Dryden urged. "Is your son in some sort of difficulty with the police? Please don't be embarrassed; I deal with all sorts of…"

"Daniel is dead."

In the heavy silence, they heard the distant thrum of traffic on the main road outside, and snatched conversation as people passed by Dryden's window.

"I'm very sorry to hear it," he said, looking between them. "Was there some sort of clinical negligence?"

James shook his head, although, in truth, there might have been. He wouldn't know, because the authorities would tell them *nothing*.

"Daniel was murdered in October, last year," he said, forcing the words from his mouth. "He was attacked and beaten to death on our estate, as he was on his way home from football practice."

Something sparked in Dryden's memory.

Nkosi.

Daniel Nkosi.

"I remember reading about the incident, at the time," he said. "I don't recall anybody having been prosecuted?"

James closed his eyes, and shook his head. "No, that's just it. The police...it seems they've done nothin'. They say there's no witnesses, but the man who lives on the third floor? He told me himself, he saw who did it. He saw *three* of them—" The words were tumbling out of his mouth, but he couldn't stop. "The police say they found drugs or somethin' on my son's body," he continued. "I tell you, he wasn't that kind of boy. *He wasn't that kind*. Ask anyone, they'll tell you. I know what they're sayin' now, because I read the newspapers. They called him a 'black drug dealer'. Why does it matter what colour his skin was? How did they know about any drugs the police found, eh? Who told them *that*?"

Dryden continued to listen, and took swift notes on an A4 pad.

"The police say they have no clues, no leads," James said, angrily. "They're lyin' to us, that's what they're doin'. I know the rumours runnin' round the estate, and the same names keep comin' up. The same three names."

"And they are?" Dryden asked.

"Paul Flint, Andrew Cobb and Zachary White," James spat. "Scum, is what they are."

Dryden recognised the first name immediately. "Did the police recover any forensic evidence or CCTV from the crime scene, or the vicinity?"

"I don' know."

Dryden looked up, then back down at his pad. "They never interviewed or confiscated any clothing or other items from the three you mentioned? No arrests were made?"

"Nothin' that we know of," James said, wearily. "They said hearsay evidence doesn't count."

Dryden sucked in a long breath, then let it whistle out again through his teeth. "Have you requested to see the police file?"

"Many times," James said. "They keep promisin', but they never send us anythin'."

Dryden put his pen down, and faced them squarely. "Tell me what you'd like me to do," he said.

"We want *answers*," James said. "We want justice for Daniel. It seems, from everythin' we've seen and heard, the police haven't investigated properly. I don' know for sure, but there's got to be some reason for that. Maybe the colour of his skin, or maybe some other reason, but I want to know what it is. I want to stop this happenin' to anyone else. I want those men—those *boys*—to be punished for what they did."

Dryden thought of all the hassle and rigmarole, the red tape and hours of administrative work that would be required to even begin cracking the hardened shell of the Metropolitan Police. He thought of Paul Flint, the notorious leader of a local white supremacy gang, and known drug dealer. It was very probable the police were covering for him, and themselves, by brushing Daniel Nkosi's murder under the mat, which meant there was the potential for a *lot* of trouble, if he so much as touched the case.

Then, he saw the brown envelope.

"What's that?"

James took out a single piece of paper. "It's the outcome of the complaint we made to the Police Complaints Authority," James said. "They said there was no case to answer, and no right of review or appeal."

Dryden held out a hand, and skim read the document. "They said all this, despite not having given you sight of the police file, or any pertinent details of what happened on the night your son died?"

They both nodded.

"Well," he said, smoothing out the piece of printed paper. "There are options, here. The police haven't indicated any suspects, made arrests or put forward anything for the Crown Prosecution Service to consider, but *you* could bring a private prosecution against the three you've mentioned—if we can put together a strong enough case."

"We don't have that kind of money," James said.

"Is there anyone who could help? I could offer part of my fees on a no-win, no-fee basis."

"The church," Irene whispered to her husband. "The church might help us."

"This won't be an easy road," Dryden cautioned them. "And there's a long way to go. I have to warn you, even *if* we manage to procure any meaningful evidence or witness statements, that doesn't mean the case we put together will be strong enough to take to court, or strong enough to win."

They nodded.

"The best thing to do now is to take some time to think about whether you'd like to proceed, and whether you can fund the costs."

"Thank you, Mr Dryden."

After they left, shuffling out of his office like broken mannequins, he thought of all the other cases of unsolved murders in that part of London. The Nkosis weren't the first family to come to him seeking justice for their dead sons and daughters, when the police had given them none. There were too many young black men, in particular, being stopped and searched for no good reason except that they 'looked the type' to be carrying drugs. There were too many unsolved cases of unlawful death, especially when the victim was a person of colour. It wasn't right, and things needed to change.

Dryden knew all of this, and yet, he was frightened.

He could admit that, privately.

He'd scraped a living all these years chasing ambulances, churning out divorce papers and conveying cheap houses, but he'd always yearned for that *big case*. The one that would change everything, and change him. He didn't have nearly enough information to know whether the Nkosi case was worth pursuing, but his gut told him it was, and so was Paul Flint.

They just needed to prove it.

CHAPTER 14

London, Present Day

Chief Constable Porter had assigned the running of OPERATION GREENWICH to one of his most experienced DCIs in Major Crimes, a woman by the name of Kathleen Verrill. She'd been with the department for almost twenty-five years and, like any other professional woman who'd risen through the police ranks, had probably faced all manner of unreported misogyny along the way. Porter didn't condone it, but nor could he deny that it still existed, in some quarters.

"All right, settle down," he said, to the room at large. "I'm going to hand over to DCI Verrill in a moment but, before then, you might have noticed a couple of new faces in the crowd. Doctor Alexander Gregory and Professor Bill Douglas have agreed to come on board as consultant profilers to assist us in the running of this case—"

There were a couple of mutters around the room, and a few derisive looks.

"—*and* I know you'll extend them a warm welcome," Porter finished, on a warning note. "We're all working together, as a team, to return an eight-year-old boy to his family. Let's not lose sight of that goal."

His eye passed over each of them, and then he took a seat.

"Thank you, Chief Constable," Verrill said, stepping forward. "You should all be aware of the facts, by now, but, for those who've been living under a rock, let me refresh your memory."

She moved to a long whiteboard, which bore a collection of scribbled notes as well as a number of printed images tacked beside them.

"This is Rory Smythe," she said, and pointed to a photograph. "He disappeared from his home in Greenwich sometime between seven-thirty and eleven-thirty, last night. There were no signs of forced entry, and his mother, father and elder brother were all in the house, at the time. His departure wasn't picked up on any of the working cameras at the house, either. So, what does this mean?"

She stuck her hands in the pockets of her trouser suit.

"Our best working theory is that Rory left the house of his own accord, though we still aren't sure how—"

"Dr Gregory has a theory about the exit route," Porter remarked, and all heads swivelled in his direction.

"Oh?" Verrill sought Gregory's face amongst the crowd.

Alex cleared his throat. "I understand the back door of the Smythe's house is the only remaining exit route that isn't covered by CCTV, as it leads onto the western elevation of the house where the camera was recently broken. However, the back door was found locked on the inside and Mrs Smythe is adamant it was already locked when she checked it?"

Verrill nodded. "That's right."

"In that case, it seems obvious Rory used the dog flap," he said. "It's the perfect size for a boy of eight, and would explain how the back door remained locked from the inside—simply, because he didn't use it."

"I can't believe we missed that," she said, echoing Porter's earlier thoughts. Verrill turned back to the room at large. "As for those of you who worked the Smythe house last night, and didn't think of that glaringly obvious explanation, consider yourselves skating on thin ice," she said, with a touch of levity. "Now, back to our working theory. If Rory left the house via the dog flap, he wouldn't have been caught on any camera on that side of the house because, as we've just said, the camera is broken. That exit leads directly to a side gate in the garden, which is protected by the same intercom system as the front driveway gates but can be opened using a code known to the family and their staff. Rory's mother has confirmed that he was aware of the code, which, she admitted, they haven't changed in over two years."

Kathleen didn't bother to remark on how things might have been very different if they had; if there was one thing she'd learned during her tenure as a detective, it was not to become too emotionally invested in a case, even ones concerning children. Allowing herself to wonder 'what if' would be sheer indulgence, and distracting from the job at hand.

"Rory doesn't have a mobile phone, nor any social media accounts, gaming accounts or an e-mail address other than the one used at school, which we've already accessed and checked," she continued. "As far as we know, there were no communications made to him digitally, so we must assume whoever lured him from the house did so verbally, at some earlier time."

She folded her arms across her chest.

"We know this isn't a case of Rory having run away, because Jonathan Smythe received a ransom e-mail at exactly midnight seeking a hundred thousand pounds in bitcoin," she said. "Digital Forensics are working to trace the source of the e-mail, but it's proving difficult and will take some time, because whoever sent it obviously knows a bit about covering themselves. So, while the tech team focus their energies on that, we'll focus on what we do best, which is old-fashioned detection."

She picked up a sheaf of printed papers, and waggled it.

"You should each have one of these packs," she said. "If you turn to page four, you'll find a list of all the people who've visited the Smythe family home, while Rory was there, over the past month—this is to the best of his parents' recollection."

Alex and Bill procured a copy, flipped to the relevant page, and noticed that the names covered a number of Anita's personal friends, some of Jonathan's work colleagues including Henry Gardiner, and several of Rory's school friends and their parents who had come for dinner or to play at the weekend. Jonathan's ex-wife, Camilla, had been to the house a number of times, including to drop Theo off for the Christmas holidays, but the number of visits nonetheless seemed unusually high for a former spouse.

"Eighty per cent of the people on that list are coming in for scheduled interviews from three o'clock onwards," Verrill told them, and glanced at the clock on the wall which told her it was quarter-to the hour. "I've assigned interviewers, and you know who you are. I want that list whittled down to anyone without an alibi for the relevant time period, and anyone who might need the money or have some other motive."

She shoved back a strand of short, shaggy blonde hair that fell into her eyes.

"As for the rest of you, continue digging into any political motivations," she said. "I want to know about anybody with a grudge, or a reason to want Jonathan Smythe compromised in this way. Keep chasing local businesses for camera footage, and, *for God's sake*, light a fire up the arse of Transport for London and get me some dash-cam footage from the buses on Greenwich High Street."

There were nods around the room.

"Doctor Gregory, Professor Douglas? Do you have anything to add?"

Heads turned again.

"In our view, the manner in which Rory was taken would suggest a non-violent perpetrator, and one who is methodical and highly organised," Bill said. "That isn't always determinative of how they will treat him, or rule out the possibility of escalating aggression if their demands aren't met, but it's something to bear in mind as regards personality type when you're conducting interviews."

Verrill nodded. "Take note of that," she said to the others in the room.

"A couple of other things," Alex put in. "Firstly, the lack of deadline in the ransom note. Any serious kidnapper would have given a firm timescale, to keep things moving along. That could indicate the perp is unsophisticated, or it could be their first time perpetrating this kind of offence. On the other hand, it could indicate more of a personal motivation than a financial one, despite the demand for money."

"What kind of personal motivation?"

"We don't know, yet," he replied. "But I'd look closely at Jonathan's ex-wife, and at any ex-business partners or other friends who might feel disgruntled."

"All right," Verrill said. "That gives us something to work with."

"Don't forget the stars," Gregory added. "Rory loves astronomy, and he can see Greenwich Observatory from his room. Anybody who knows him would know that, and could use it."

"Do you think they're acting alone, or with an accomplice?" Verrill asked.

"Too early to say," he replied. "I'd put my money on there being more than one, because one party will need to be visible while the other looks after Rory, behind the scenes. Likewise, the silent partner might have been the one to snatch Rory, or lead him willingly to the place where he's now being held, while the other was alibied by witnesses."

Verrill turned to the whiteboard and considered the young boy smiling back at her. His mother was pushing to go public with the news that her son was missing, so that well-meaning people could help to search for him. Her husband took a different view, and it was one she happened to share, which was that going public too early could place undue pressure on a kidnapper and lead them to take rash decisions. As a mother herself, she understood both sides and the imperative to *act*, but she recalled Gregory's point about the perpetrator possibly being new to the game. First timers were far more likely to act in haste, and with untold consequences.

"All right," she said, turning back to the room. "It's almost three o'clock, so let's get moving. I want to hear from all of you with an update by six, this evening—and, before you start squawking about overtime, it's already been approved."

Before Alex and Bill could join the exodus back along the corridor, DCI Verrill caught up with them.

"Thank you for your insights, there," she said. "Sometimes, we can be too close to the problem to see the wood for the trees."

"In our business, too," Bill said, magnanimously. "Thank you for being so cooperative."

"I'm a parent," she explained. "No matter what my feelings are about criminal profiling or its efficacy, I know that, if this was my child,

I'd want as many people working to try and find him as possible." She looked between them, and seemed satisfied with what she saw. "Look, you said you'd be interested in what Camilla Smythe has to say? Well, she's one of my interviewees, in about five minutes. You're welcome to come down to the interview suite and observe—I'd be interested to know your impressions of her, and some of the others who've agreed to come in and give a statement."

"Thank you, we'd appreciate it."

They set off down the corridor towards the lift, which would take them down into the bowels of Scotland Yard.

CHAPTER 15

Camilla Smythe had chosen to keep her married name.

It was a small point, but an interesting one, nonetheless. Usually, divorcees tended to revert to their maiden name following the *decree absolute*, but, for some reason, Camilla had chosen not to. There hadn't been any scope to question either Anita or Jonathan Smythe about the circumstances of his divorce, but, it seemed DCI Verrill had no qualms in addressing the most awkward of subject matters.

"Ms Smythe," she began, once Camilla had seated herself at one of the small, four-seater tables in the interview suite. "I want to thank you again for agreeing to come in; as you can imagine, this is a worrying time for your ex-husband and his wife."

Camilla was dressed entirely in premium workout gear, from her leggings to the slim-fitting Lycra jacket in a contrasting shade of hot pink. The outfit showed off an extremely slim physique, which had been toned and sculpted to within an inch of its life thanks to an impressive schedule of reformer Pilates and weights training. Her blonde hair was styled around an attractive face which, in their best estimation, was probably somewhere in its early fifties, give or take a few nips and tucks. In other words, she was everything they'd imagined she would be.

"She looks an awful lot like—"

"Anita?" Bill whispered, as he and Alex watched the interview through the observation window. "I was just thinking the same thing. Camilla's a slightly older version, but Smythe certainly has a type."

"We don't know any of the circumstances," Alex said, keeping his voice low. "But, if Jonathan had an affair, or perhaps just wanted a younger model, that's exactly the kind of thing that would cause deep-rooted resentment in his ex-wife.

Especially so, if his new wife happens to look like a younger version of herself."

"It'd be a kick in the teeth," Bill agreed.

They fell silent, and listened to the two women on the other side of the glass.

"It's no trouble," Camilla was saying. "I'm obviously devastated to hear about poor little Rory. He's such a *sweetie*, too. He looks a lot like Theo did, at that age…" She grabbed her glass of water, and took a long gulp. "Anyway, I'm happy to help," she said.

"Thank you," Verrill said, and folded her hands on top of the table. "We're asking the same questions of many people, Ms Smythe, and the first one is: what were you doing last night, between the hours of seven-thirty and eleven-thirty?"

Camilla raised a single, well-shaped eyebrow. "Ah, well, let me see. My Pilates class finished at six-thirty, and I had a green juice with the girls at the health club, afterwards, so I didn't leave until around seven-fifteen. I walked home from the club—"

"Which is where?" Verrill interjected.

"Oh, it's just beside the Maritime Museum," she replied.

Verrill paused to look at a map on her phone, and saw that it was less than ten minutes' walk from the Smythe residence. She also happened to know that Camilla still lived in the old family home, which was within close proximity, on the other side of the park and the observatory. The route home from her Pilates class would have taken her within striking distance of Rory, and well within the timeframe he was taken.

"Around what time did you arrive home?" she asked.

"It must have been around half past seven," Camilla replied. "It isn't far."

"Did you happen to see anyone you recognise, or anything unusual, on your way?"

Camilla sighed, and shook her head. "Believe me, I've been racking my brains to try to remember *anything* that could help," she replied. "But, the fact is, I was in my own little world, just walking home and looking forward to a hot bath and a bit of *Outlander*."

Verrill decided to switch track. "Tell me about your relationship with Mr Smythe and his wife," she said. "I understand you were divorced some time ago?"

Camilla couldn't quite hide the flicker of irritation that passed over her face. "Yes," she said, very calmly. "Jonathan and I parted ways when Theo was four. We've co-parented very well since then."

Verrill waited, drawing out the silence, until Camilla was compelled to fill it.

"Well, you know," she said, flapping her hand. "It was difficult, at first. No woman likes to find out her husband's been having an affair with the nanny, do they?"

"Was Anita your family nanny?"

Camilla's mouth flattened, and she gave a brief nod.

"Believe it or not, I was the fool who hired her," she muttered, but then, in a flash, she was all smiles again. "You know what they say, though. Better to know the truth than to live a lie. I'm sure we're all much, *much* happier now."

Verrill didn't believe a word of it, but she smiled along.

"That's a very positive attitude to take," she said, then leaned forward conspiratorially. "Now, if it were *me*, I'd have wanted to string my husband up from the nearest tree."

Camilla looked shocked, then she gave a nervous laugh. "I can't say I haven't imagined a few scenarios," she admitted. "But, what's done is done, isn't it? And, I'd certainly *never* wish for anything like this to happen."

"Do you know of anyone who might?"

Camilla shook her head. "No, certainly nobody of *my* acquaintance," she said. "I can't speak for Anita. One never knows what circles she moved in, before meeting Jonathan." She gulped some more water. "But, that sounded unkind. All I mean to say is, while Jonathan and I were married, I helped to build his political career. We moved in the same social circles, we knew the same people, and our lives were entwined. Anita was an outsider, and lived a very different sort of life before her fortunes turned.

There may be all kinds of skeletons that even Jonathan doesn't know about."

Verrill nodded. "I understand—we'll be sure to look into things thoroughly."

"Please do," Camilla urged her. "As you can imagine, I've been worrying about Theo. Do you think I should bring him home?"

"That's a matter between you and Mr Smythe," Verrill replied. "However, we have twenty-four-hour surveillance over his property, now, so there's very little scope for there to be a repeat of last night's events."

"Oh, you have? That's such a comfort to know."

"Are you seeing anyone at the moment, Ms Smythe?"

Camilla was caught off-guard. "Me? Oh…do you really need to know that?"

Verrill nodded. "If you don't mind."

"Well, it's nothing serious," Camilla replied. "But, I met someone online—" She closed her eyes, as if she'd just confessed to murder. "I never thought I'd be someone to use an online dating app, not at my age," she said, in a pained voice. "What's the world coming to? But…anyway,

I thought I'd give it a try. There were a few no-hopers, I can tell you, but then I found Alan. He's going through a divorce, so he's not ready for any major commitment, but we see one another from time to time."

Verrill took down his name and address. "Were you with Alan last night?"

"No, not last night," Camilla replied. "I was on my own, since Theo is away." *And felt incredibly lonely,* she might have added. "It was a great opportunity to catch up with some reading, and my favourite shows, rather than having to put up with whatever Theo wants to watch."

"And what does Theo like?"

"Oh, all the Marvel films, obviously," she said. "Anything sci-fi, futuristic, or dystopian. I can't stand any of that. Give me *Bridget Jones* or *My Fair Lady* any day of the week."

Verrill happened to agree with her, but that was an aside. "We understand you've paid a number of visits to Mr and Mrs Smythe's home, over the past month," she continued. "Could you tell me why?"

"To discuss Theo, naturally," Camilla said, a bit defensively. "We do still share a child, Chief Inspector."

Verrill reached for her paperwork, and took her time counting the number of visits. "You paid a total of eleven house calls, which averages at around three visits per week."

"Does it?" Camilla said. "Well, I wasn't keeping count."

"Would you care to tell me what required so much discussion?"

"That's a private matter, between Jonathan and myself," she said. "It has nothing to do with Rory's disappearance—"

"With respect, Ms Smythe, I'll be the judge of that."

Camilla refolded her arms. "*Fine*," she hissed. "I've been...well, I suppose I've been drinking a bit more than usual, lately. It's been suggested by my doctor that I might... I might benefit from a short stay at a kind of... *health farm* to wean me off it, a bit, and get me back on track. I'm afraid I'd had a few glasses of wine, when I went to Jonathan and Anita's, and I made a bit of a fool of myself. Are you happy now?"

"Thank you for your candour, Ms Smythe."

In the observation room, Gregory turned to his friend.

"Do you believe her?"

Bill continued to study the woman on the other side of the glass, and then shook his head slowly.

"No," he said. "I don't think I've believed a single word she's said throughout the interview, and yet, it's all believable."

"The police will check her story out," Alex said. "But, that doesn't help us right now. By her own admission, she knows Rory, has crossed paths with him several times this month, and was in the area last night. She could have collected Rory from the side entrance as she was on her way home."

"It's been ten years, and she's still angry about her husband's infidelity," Bill said. "That's a long time for anger to grow, and fantasies about revenge to build. The question is whether her fantasies crossed over into reality—especially with some alcohol to boost her confidence."

Alex nodded. "That being said, Camilla doesn't strike me as someone who'd be particularly adept at sending untraceable e-mails."

"She could have had help," Bill mused. "But, there's a long list of potential suspects. Let's keep an open mind."

Alex turned back to the observation glass and watched Camilla rise to her feet, preparing to leave. He reflected that time was a strange concept; for Naomi, the days were endlessly long, punctuated by small milestones such as opening her eyes. For Rory Smythe, time was accelerating with every passing minute, slipping away like sand.

CHAPTER 16

Three hours later, the police team gathered in the conference room once again, looking considerably less energetic than before. DCI Verrill had ordered a strategic caffeine injection for her staff, and there were murmurs of approval as a couple of constables came in bearing trays of steaming coffee.

She thanked them, then took a scalding sip which she regretted immediately.

Would she never learn?

"Right," she said, swallowing. "Let's see what progress has been made."

Verrill took out a pen, and moved over to one of the empty whiteboards.

"I want to see everything written up on the system by the end of the day but, for now, let's stick to the old-fashioned methods."

She scrawled, 'CAMILLA SMYTHE' on the board, and turned to face the room again.

"As you all know, Camilla is Jonathan Smythe's ex-wife, and mother to his eldest son, Theo, who is seventeen," she said. "When giving her statement, she revealed that she had no alibi for last night, between the hours of seven-thirty and eleven-thirty. In fact, she also admitted she would have passed within a couple of hundred yards of the Smythe house, while on her way home from a Pilates class. That puts her in the area at around seven-thirty, which is when Anita Smythe put Rory to bed. It would have been easy enough for Camilla to hang around and meet the boy after that time, in the alleyway behind the garden gate."

She scrawled a few notes next to the woman's name.

"As for motive, she told us she has a drink problem," Verrill said. "Whether that's true or not, we don't know, but we can't be sure there aren't money worries, too. As for her general attitude towards the family, she claimed to like the boy, but harbours obvious resentment towards both Anita and Jonathan Smythe, whom she claims was adulterous at the time their marriage broke down."

She noted that down on the board, alongside a few more pertinent details.

"My next interviewee was the family housekeeper, Stefanie King," Verrill said. "She'd already given a statement to our first responding officers, but was very cooperative."

She wrote the woman's name next to Camilla's, and twiddled the pen in her hands.

"Stefanie is thirty-two, unmarried, and lives on her own in a rented flat in Lewisham," she said. "She's worked for the Smythe family for five years, and, when she isn't working three days a week for them, she does an Art and Design course at the Fashion College."

Verrill paused to take another sip of coffee, scalded her mouth again, and muttered something rude beneath her breath.

"Stefanie had finished work by the time Rory went missing," she said. "Her usual hours are between seven and four, which means she's there in the morning to help with breakfasts and tends to prepare the evening meal before she leaves."

Gregory thought he heard somebody mutter that it was 'all right for some'.

"Stefanie tells us that she went straight home after work, stopping off at the supermarket for some provisions," Verrill said. "As it happens, we've already confirmed that she made the stop, from the CCTV footage provided by Tesco on the high street. Therefore, we can place Stefanie King at Tesco Metro between four-thirty-five and four-fifty-two. After that, we know she continued along the high street, but we can't place her anywhere else, after that time."

Verrill tapped the board.

"Which, of course, means that Stefanie also has no alibi for the relevant timeframe," she said. "Moreover, she is very familiar with Rory, who's known her since he was three years old."

"Does she have a partner?" Gregory asked, and waited for the inevitable head-swivelling in his direction.

"She says not, however, interestingly, Anita Smythe seemed to think Stefanie had a man on the scene somewhere," Verrill said. She remarked on it, in passing."

She turned back to the board.

"We've already confirmed that Smythe's driver, Gordon Jenkins, is alibied for the timeframe, but that doesn't mean he isn't accomplice to a crime or that he doesn't know anything about it. Tindell? What did you make of him, when you took his statement?"

She listened while one of her staff described the interview, which had been straightforward, and then moved to the next person on her list.

"Henry Gardiner," she declared. "Smythe's closest parliamentary aide, and a man with personal, detailed knowledge of their family's routine, as well as having a good relationship with Rory. Apparently, his son, David, goes to the same school and they play together. That's a relationship of trust on several levels."

"According to Gardiner, he was having a few after-work bevvies at the bar between six and eight-thirty," one of the team said. "After that, he walked home along the Embankment towards Putney, where he lives with his wife and two children. His wife confirms he got home around ten o'clock."

"Which still leaves plenty of time for him to have hopped in a taxi and gone to Greenwich, instead," Verrill noted. "Or, to have been a partner to Rory's disappearance, if not the person who collected him."

"Have the Smythes ever received any threatening letters before?" Bill asked.

"None, aside from the usual letters from constituents who aren't happy with his performance at PMQs," Verrill replied. "Why do you ask?"

"The ransom note seemed amateurish, as we said earlier. Gardiner presents as a man more than capable of crafting a professional threat, if he wanted to."

"Unless he didn't want the note to sound like he'd written it," Verrill replied, and Bill inclined his head. "The fact is, we've got several key people with means and opportunity, and potential motives as yet to be uncovered. It doesn't bring us any closer to finding Rory, so I've ordered covert surveillance on the three people we've mentioned, and we'll see where that gets us."

Gregory listened, and found himself wondering, 'why now?'

All of the people under surveillance had known Anita and Jonathan Smythe for several years, and Rory for just as long. It was curious that they should wait all that time before executing a kidnap plan, unless there was some outside imperative that compelled them to act now.

"Are you looking into their financials?" he asked.

"Requests have been made of their banks," Verrill replied. "We're waiting for the information to filter through."

Gregory wondered how much longer Rory Smythe could wait.

CHAPTER 17

Xavier House, 1997

Two years after Daniel's death

Ava Nkosi slipped a tray of fish fingers and chips into the oven and set the chicken-shaped timer for twenty-five minutes. That would give her enough time to change out of her school uniform and clean the bathroom, before putting dinner on the table. There was some laundry to do, which meant dragging a canvas bag down to the basement launderette, and she'd been hoping one of her parents might have remembered to do it so that she didn't have to brave the scariest part of the building and strain her arms in the process.

Unfortunately, they hadn't.

They hadn't remembered to take the rubbish out, either, which meant that she'd come home to the unpleasantly ripe smell of rotting vegetables.

At least it covered the smell of whisky, she thought.

At twelve years old, she'd lived through her own grief since Daniel died but, unlike James and Irene, it was not merely her brother she mourned. She missed having two functional parents who laughed, sang, and remembered she existed. She missed having a mother she could talk to, especially since she'd started menstruating the week before and had been frightened. She missed having a father who played board games and helped with her maths homework, or made her an omelette once in a while.

It was lucky her father was still employed, but Ava was wise enough to know that, if he continued drinking as he was, he would soon be unfit to continue managing the sales team at the electronics store, as he had done for the past fifteen years. Customers didn't like to smell alcohol when they came in to buy a television.

As for her mother...
She'd found God.

Oh, they'd always gone to church every Sunday, and sang hymns, clapped and danced and listened to harmless sermons about kindness and fables from the Bible about loving thy neighbour. Ava didn't mind any of that, even if she didn't *really* believe there was a big, all-powerful God somewhere out there. But now, her mum went to church every day, to pray, to volunteer, to pray some more...there was talk of her being baptised *again*.

Ava looked around the living room walls, which had once featured some framed watercolour prints by Monet, but had been replaced with a series of embroidered passages from the Bible. A large, wooden effigy of Christ on the cross hung above the gas fireplace beside a single framed image of Daniel.

Ava felt a sharp stab of pain in her chest as she looked into her brother's kind, brown eyes, and looked away quickly, unwilling to cry when there was so much to be done.

Ava had dinner ready by the time James and Irene arrived home. He, from his habitual thrice-weekly trip to Mr Ali's, and she, from her daily visit to church. Neither of them noticed that the rubbish had been removed, or the carpets vacuumed; they'd found their own way to cope with Daniel's loss, and to continue living each day without him. There was only one subject matter on which they agreed, and that was the private prosecution.

The paperwork that had been accumulated in the year since they'd first paid a visit to Alfie Dryden's office covered the dining table. Ava had learned never to touch the neat piles, and so the three of them balanced a plate of fish fingers, chips and peas on their laps in the living area, instead. They ate in silence, until Ava tried to spark a conversation.

"Mum? How was church today?"

Irene continued to eat, her mind elsewhere.

"I—I had a good day at school," Ava ventured, when no reply was forthcoming. "The teacher thinks I should enter this poetry competition. The winner gets a thousand pounds, and their poem published."

James looked up at the mention of money. "What's that? A thousand pounds for what, now?"

"It's a prize," Ava explained. "If I win the poetry competition."

James grunted, and returned to his meal, wondering how many billable hours that would buy them for Daniel's case.

"How's the fundraising comin' along?" he asked his wife.

Ava sighed inwardly, and knew that all chance of conversation was now over. The two of them would discuss the next steps until nightfall, back and forth, until her mother went to bed, exhausted, and her father stayed up drinking and speaking to Daniel's photograph. Often, he fell asleep in the easy chair, and needed to be roused the following morning before he was late for work.

"It's coming along," Irene said, excitedly. "They've hit five thousand, now, so we only need another two or three to be able to carry on and hire the barrister."

"We need more publicity," James said. "There's a new MP in now, so I think we should try speakin' to them. They can't be any worse than the last one."

Ava stood up, and began clearing away their plates.

"I'll make an appointment tomorrow," Irene said.

"I saw 'im today," James said, darkly.

"Who's that?"

"Him. The one wit' the scar. He looked me in the eye, bold as brass."

Irene's lip quivered. "God is good," she said. "He won't forsake us, or Daniel. He'll get what's coming to him, from the Almighty, James. We just need to carry on doing what we're doing. We have to have faith in the justice system."

Unlike his wife, James hadn't turned to any deity for solace.

"Sometimes, you have to *make* justice happen," he said, and looked across at his son.

Ava watched them from the doorway, and then disappeared down the corridor to her room, to complete her homework. If she could only win that poetry competition, maybe that would make her parents happier. If she could only do the laundry and keep the house clean and tidy, that would make their lives easier. If she could only find whoever killed her brother, and—

And—

Kill them, her mind whispered.

Afraid of her own thoughts, Ava hurried to her room and hid beneath the covers of her bed, wishing her mother would come and stroke her hair, as she used to.

While Ava hid from the monsters in her mind, DI Lipman and DS Vaughn stood on the banks of the Thames, not far from New Scotland Yard. They lit a couple of cigarettes and took a few drags, before turning to business.

"The take was down last month," Lipman began.

"Same as the month before," Vaughn said. "Apparently, Flint says gear is gettin' cheaper. Supply is outstrippin' demand, for once, and they've had to slash prices. He's had his boys givin' away a bit for free, to get people hooked, then he'll call in the debt down the line but it's a loss-leader at the moment."

Lipman nodded, and tapped the ash from the end of his cigarette.

"Speaking of our friend Flinty," he said. "You heard anything more about that kid—Daniel Nkosi?"

Vaughn took a long drag, and shook his head. "All quiet, for now," he said. "I think we've stitched that one up, well enough. The family aren't givin' up, mind you. They put that complaint in, last year."

"Which was rejected," Lipman said, with a tigerish smile. "Funny, that."

Vaughn laughed. "Yeah. Even if they tried anythin' else, they'd only look like a couple of bad parents tryin' to bring down hardworkin' officers," he said. "That piece in the paper from your old friend Derek did the trick, didn't it? Their son's not some innocent lad, in the eyes of the public; he's a drug dealer, who got his comeuppance. Throw in the fact he's mixed, and Bob's your uncle. There's nothin' easier than playin' the public."

Lipman nodded. "I heard the father's hit the bottle hard," he said. "That won't help with the family's credibility, will it?"

Vaughn shook his head, and then frowned. "D' you remember the girl?"

"What girl?"

"The daughter—the Nkosi's daughter."

Lipman nodded, remembering her serious brown eyes.

"I dunno why, but she bothered me," Vaughn said. "Somethin' about the way she looked at us."

He stubbed out his cigarette, and rubbed his hands together.

"You're getting soft," Lipman said, but he remembered the look in that girl's eyes, and it made him shiver.

CHAPTER 18

London, Present Day

Ava saw a room with cream-painted walls and a double bed, neatly made. Along one of the walls, she saw a long black line with dates and names written beside it, and photographs pinned above it. Below that was a series of acrostic letters written along the left side, paired with surnames on the right.

VINDICTA SERVIVIT FRIGUS, the acrostic read.

Somebody had circled the 'I's in green pen.

Her foot touched something solid, and she looked down to find a woman lying sprawled at her feet, face-down in the carpet. The back of her head was badly wounded, and blood seeped into her dark hair.

In her dream, Ava let out a strangled cry and stumbled back in horror.

Tut, tut, a man's voice said.

She looked up to find the barrel of a gun pointed at her head.

There was no time to run, before—

Bang!

Ava woke up with a scream, covered in a film of sweat.

Breathing hard, heart hammering against her chest, she slowly became aware of her surroundings.

A hospital bed.

She was in hospital, after the attack.

She had amnesia.

"You all right, love?"

The woman in the bed to her right spoke through the privacy curtain.

"I—I'm—yes, I'm alright," she said. "Sorry to have woken you up."

"I'm a light sleeper, anyhow," the woman said. "Do you want me to call a nurse?"

"No, no, I'll be fine," Ava said.

"Okie dokie," came the reply. "You should think about eatin' a banana before bed, you know. They're supposed to be just the thing for peaceful dreams."

On which note, the woman turned over and, a minute later, Ava heard her rumbling snores. She lay there listening to them while her heart rate returned to normal, and then reached across to the journal beside her bed to make some notes about the dream she'd had. When it was done, she checked the time on her mobile phone.

Three forty-seven.

Too early to be awake, but too late to fall back asleep.

Ava closed her eyes, and immediately found herself looking down the barrel of a gun again.

Her eyes flew open.

Unsettled, she swung her legs out of the bed and lowered herself to the floor as quietly as she could. She had the choice of a Zimmer frame or a walking stick and, on that occasion, she chose the stick. She shoved her feet into a pair of slippers, wrapped herself in the terry towelling robe her mother had brought from home, and set off down the corridor.

Ava passed the nurse's station, where a young woman of nineteen or twenty was seated with her head propped against her hand.

Spotting her, the nurse came to attention.

"Is everything all right?" she asked. "Do you need something?"

Ava shook her head. "Just having a bit of trouble sleeping," she explained. "I thought I'd go for a walk, to tire myself out."

"Oh," the nurse replied. "Well, that's a good idea, so long as you don't overdo it—"

"I won't," Ava assured her, with a smile.

She continued along the corridor and glanced back to the nurse's station to find that it was now unoccupied, the young staff nurse having gone to the bathroom or to make a cup of tea. She bypassed the lifts in favour of the stairwell beside them and slowly, painstakingly, lowered herself down the steps until she reached the floor below, where long-term intensive care patients slept.

Ava pushed open the door from the stairwell and checked the corridor, but heard nothing except the thrum of machinery and the dim chatter of nurses. Suddenly, an alarm sounded, and she ducked back into the stairwell as footsteps clattered along the corridor towards whichever emergency demanded attention. Once they were gone, she stepped out into the corridor and made her way in the opposite direction, where the private rooms were numbered between one and twenty on that side of the hospital, just as they were on the floor above.

Presently, she came to a door marked '15'.

She leaned on her walking stick and peered through the window to see a woman with dark hair lying perfectly still, surrounded by monitors.

Tut, tut, a voice said.

Ava's head whipped around, but there was nobody there.

She looked back at Naomi Palmer, then returned to the stairwell.

Detective Sergeant Ben Carter couldn't sleep, either.

In contrast to the persona he'd created around The Yard, his flat was an oasis of calm colours and spotless surfaces, without an errant crumb in sight. He appreciated method and order, and had no time for a cluttered space nor a cluttered mind.

Which was precisely why he couldn't sleep.

He'd spent hours going back over the files he'd amassed in the three years he'd been investigating Ava Hope—or Ava Nkosi, as she was formerly known—and had almost driven himself mad trying to find something, *anything* that he'd missed.

Frustrated, but unwilling to give up, he picked up the file pertaining to Carl Deere's recent suicide and the events leading up to it. *It was a sad case*, he thought. Ordinarily, he hardened himself against the criminal minds he hunted, but it was impossible not to feel a certain grudging sympathy for a man who'd lived through a traumatic childhood and gone on to live a dysfunctional existence as an adult. He'd been wrongfully convicted of multiple murders and imprisoned for years but, as it happened, being innocent of those murders hadn't stopped him from killing people once he was released. Carl Deere had gone on a spree, systematically murdering a list of people he associated with his conviction, all the while telling himself he was an angel of justice. By the time he'd come to his senses, suicide had been the only way out.

Carter flipped through the pages of the file until he came to the witness statements provided by Bill Douglas and Alex Gregory, both of whom had been present in the former's office at Hawking College, where Carl had died. He read over Gregory's statement, first, and his eye caught on a particular passage towards the end:

"We asked Carl whether there was anything else he would like to tell us, before he died. In response, Carl repeated the phrase, 'It's all in the eyes'."

Carter leaned back against the sofa as he considered this. Why would Carl Deere have said, 'It's all in the eyes'—and, why did he repeat it, more than once? Obviously, he considered it an important message to impart at that critical moment, but what did he *mean*? Whose eyes, and what message did they convey? Carter rubbed the back of his neck, and, giving up on sleep entirely, heaved himself off the sofa and walked through to the kitchen to make himself another cup of coffee.

Of course, the words could have been nonsense; just the ramblings of a dying man.

He took his coffee back to the living room and continued thumbing through the file and reading over Douglas's statement, which corroborated Gregory's account almost to the letter. Then, setting that file aside, he dusted off the next, which was a thick collection of linked files relating to the murders and attempted murders thought to have been perpetrated by the late Carl Deere. Carter spent some time going over the notes relating to the deaths, until he came to the murder of his former colleague, Detective Inspector Ian O' Shea.

Ian had only been at The Yard a few days before he was found dead in his flat, his throat having been cut. Unbeknownst to many people, Ian had been one of the undercover officers involved in Carl Deere's original entrapment, although he'd used an assumed name at the time and had been relocated to Birmingham shortly afterwards, for his own protection. Because of this, it was plausible that Deere had somehow found Ian, tracked down his new address and killed him.

However, Carter didn't think so.

For one thing, there was no record of any computer breach at The Yard that would suggest Deere had gained access to Ian's confidential files, and therefore he had no way of knowing the man's real name as opposed to the undercover name he'd used years before. For another, Ian had only recently moved to London, so it would have been an extreme coincidence, or stroke of good fortune, for Carl to have not only stumbled upon Ian in the flesh and recognised him, but also to have come by his new address. Finally, he agreed with Doctor Gregory's observations at the time, which were that the manner in which Ian died was inconsistent with Deere's usual MO. It lacked a 'message'—a book, a letter, or some other item left as a calling card on the body, and the execution was done from behind, whereas Carl considered it a point of principle to kill each of his victims face-to-face.

Ava Hope, on the other hand...

They'd begun a relationship, of sorts, and therefore her DNA had good reason to be all over his flat—which, very conveniently, eliminated her from suspicion in the eyes of the forensic team. Ava found out Ian was part of the original investigative team when Carl was imprisoned, but had no idea he'd worked undercover. Therefore, when she asked him about it, Ian stuck to protocol and said nothing about his involvement, which caused her to form the baseless assumption that he was lying to her, and the only possible reason was because he was a member of the Ghost Squad.

Guilty minds saw guilty deeds.

Carter moved onto a photograph of the scene at Douglas's house in Cambridge, where Ava and Naomi had been attacked. He saw Gregory's acrostic theory in the background, written on the wall, with a number of letters written along the left-hand side spelling out the Latin phrase, VINDICTA SERVIVIT FRIGUS.

Revenge served cold.

He thought again of Ava Hope, and of the revenge she'd taken for herself.

It had been ice cold.

He reached for one of the older files sitting on the table, one labelled 'Daniel Nkosi'. It was an abridged file he'd personally printed and bound for his own reference, all of the details being readily available online if needed. However, in his game, it was far better to avoid accessing the digital files too often, just in case Ava should happen to check the log—or anyone else, for that matter. Sometimes, an over-zealous Head of IT could assume the worst, when an officer like himself accessed certain files too regularly and without any obvious reason. It aroused suspicion, and he wasn't able to defend himself without uncovering the true reason for his interest. That had happened a couple of times over the years, and got him into a bit of bother.

He flipped open the first page of Daniel's file, and found himself looking into the eyes of a young, smiling boy who'd barely had a chance to live, before he'd died a brutal death at the hands of brutal people. Their actions could never be excused, but nor could they justify Ava taking the law into her own hands.

Of course, Carter acknowledged that it was very easy for him to think in such a linear way. He'd never lost a loved one to the hands of a racist gang, and been denied justice for so long afterwards. He wasn't a hypocrite, so he couldn't say he wouldn't have sought his own revenge, or felt murderous himself. But, when all was said and done, they each chose their battle lines, and he was on the side of defending Law and Order. The coffee turned cold as Carter continued to scrutinise the old files, uncaring of how exhausted he might be later in the day.

He had three months, and he wasn't going to waste a second of them.

CHAPTER 19

The next morning

"*Anita!*"

Jonathan Smythe called out to his wife, who was sitting in the kitchen with Theo. Hearing the urgent tone, they both sprang up and hurried towards his study at the other end of the house.

"What is it, Jon? Is it Rory? Have they found him?"

One look at her husband's face told her that wasn't the case.

"It's another ransom e-mail," he said. "Theo, you don't need to hear this, go into the other room—"

"Dad, I'm seventeen," he protested.

His father passed a hand over his weary face. "Alright," he said. "This time, they're giving us twelve hours to pay, or we won't see Rory again."

Anita began to cry.

"I'm sorry, darling," Jonathan said. "I'm so sorry this has happened."

He crossed the room and put his arms around his wife, while his elder soon looked on. After a moment, he held out an arm to him, too.

"Come here," he murmured.

His son hurried over, and buried his face in his father's chest.

"I'm sorry I haven't spent more time with Rory," he mumbled. "I feel so bad about it. Maybe if we'd been closer, he'd have told me what was happening."

"Don't blame yourself," Jonathan said and, in an extraordinary display of affection, gave his son a kiss on top of his head. "If anyone's to blame, it's me. My work has brought this to our door."

"*Rory*," Anita wept. "He must be so frightened."

Jonathan gave them both one last squeeze, and then stepped away. "I have to put a call through to the Chief Constable and DCI Verrill," he said. "I'll let Gregory and Douglas know, as well."

As he moved off, Theo and Anita looked at one another.

"If you want, I can go back to my mum's house," he offered, not knowing what else to say.

Anita shook her head.

"We're happy you're with us, Theo, and your father needs you. We both do."

He fiddled with the hem of his t-shirt. "I could…get you a cup of tea?"

She didn't particularly like tea, but appreciated the gesture. "That would be lovely."

Gregory and Douglas had been awake for hours when the call came through.

"Another ransom note," Alex said to his friend. "This time, imposing a twelve-hour deadline."

Bill folded his hands across his paunch, and frowned. "I still can't understand why they would delay," he said. "Why not impose a deadline from the beginning? What are they waiting for?"

"The family are nearing the end of their rope," Alex replied. "Perhaps the objective was to cause as much heartache as possible."

"Now, that's interesting," Bill said. "If it was an experienced criminal gang, or something of that kind, there wouldn't be any particular malice towards the Smythe family. They'd see it as 'purely business' and would have been far more likely to set a deadline."

"Agreed," Alex said. "Which means our gut feeling about this being personal could prove to be correct. Unfortunately, *all* of the current suspects have a personal relationship with the Smythe family, and any one of them might have a motive to hurt them in this way."

"It could be an ideologue, trying to make a statement," Bill said.

"Smythe isn't controversial, by parliamentary standards," Alex replied. "There are others who'd satisfy that purpose far better than he does."

"Still, he sits on the Select Committee," Bill reminded him.

"But whoever is doing this wants money, not favours," Alex argued. "There's been no mention of political coercion."

Bill fell silent, thinking of the personality types they'd come across before. "Every case is so different," he said, eventually. "I was thinking of the time that baby girl was taken—you remember?"

Alex nodded. "I could hardly forget."

"Yes, it was harrowing," Bill said. "If you recall, the baby was taken by a young woman who'd suffered extreme delusions. She thought the baby was hers, and that she was simply stealing it back from those who'd taken her in the first place."

"I don't think we're dealing with psychosis, in this case," Alex said. "But, I take your point. The motivations can be so wide-ranging. On the face of it, this is a straightforward money-grab. But then, why have they waited so long? It's sloppy, and suggests an ulterior motivation." He checked the time on the wall. "I'm going to pay Ava and Naomi a visit, then I'll meet you at The Yard in time for the briefing at ten-thirty," he said.

"There's something else," Bill said, and Alex paused on his way to the door.

"What's that?"

"The kidnappers haven't sent any proof that Rory is still alive."

"Yes," Alex said. "I noticed that, too."

CHAPTER 20

London, 31st December 1999

London was giddy with excitement as it prepared to usher in a new millennium.

The streets swelled with people who'd travelled from around the world to celebrate on the riverbank, where the Mayor had thrown caution to the wind and ordered a firework display so spectacular it would never be forgotten. Ava Nkosi heard about it from her friends at school, who planned to be there with their families and everybody else, as the clock struck midnight. She imagined they were already down by the river, wrapped up in their winter coats, cold but happy to be a part of something that was bigger than themselves. She thought this, as she watched the coverage on television, the sound turned down low so as not to wake her mother who slept in the room next door. Her father still hadn't come home and, in the old days, she might have worried about that.

Not now.

James Nkosi had lost all sense of time, and all sense of himself.

He'd lost his job the previous year, too.

Remembering that, Ava turned off the television, as well as the unnecessary side lights that burned a cheap, energy-saving glow around the living room. She checked the temperature, and turned it down another couple of degrees, telling herself she'd be in bed soon and wouldn't feel the difference, anyway. As she did, there came the sound of a key in the front door and, a moment later, her father stumbled inside.

She watched him fall against the wall, and throw out a hand to stop himself.

"Dad!"

He looked up, squinting his eyes to see through the haze of alcohol and dim lighting.

"Ava," he mumbled. "My—my little Ava. C' mere, Princess. *C' mere—*"

He fell forward again and, this time, was unable to stop himself clattering into the hallway table.

Her mother hurried into the hallway. "What's all the—*oh*."

There was a wealth of meaning in that simple word, Ava thought.

"Go to bed," she told Ava. "I'll see to him."

"It's okay, Mum. I don't mind."

Irene wanted to be strong, as she used to be, but couldn't find the energy.

"Dryden says we—we haven't got enough evidence to take the case forward," James said, sliding down to the floor in a heap. "He's done his best, he says, but the Met have closed ranks."

"What?" Irene said. "*What* did you say?"

"We can'—can't take the case forward," James slurred. "He rang me. Said he was s-sorry." James began to laugh, brokenly.

Irene thought of all the hours she'd spent fundraising, and all the hope she'd poured into bringing a private prosecution against the gang members. It was all that had kept her going, since Daniel died; the only thing that had given her a sense of purpose and a reason to get up each morning.

She turned and walked back into the bedroom, shutting the door behind her.

Ava watched her mother leave and wanted to shout at her, to beg her to be the person she used to be, once upon a time. To tell her she was still here, and still breathing.

But she didn't.

She walked over to where her father lay slumped on the floor and, with a wiry strength, hooked one of his arms around her slim shoulders.

"Stand up, Dad."

"Mmfh?"

"Stand up, I can't carry you."

It took ten minutes, but she managed to get him back onto his feet. His head was lolling around his shoulders, and his feet stumbled over the carpet, so she decided to deposit him on the sofa instead of trying to make it to the bedroom. She was sweating profusely by the time they made it that far, but she still took the trouble to curl his legs into a comfortable position and to drape a blanket over his body so that he wouldn't get too cold during the night.

She also set a bucket on the floor beside the sofa, just in case.

"Goodnight, Dad," she whispered. "I—I love you."

James Nkosi didn't sleep.

After he'd heaved the contents of his stomach into the bucket his daughter left for him, he stared for a while through the semi-darkness at the picture of his son, which still rested on the mantelpiece. The photograph was already beginning to fade with time, although it felt like only yesterday when their world was forever changed.

I'm sorry, Daniel.

I'm sorry, I failed you.

Outside, the sky lit up with a thousand multicoloured fireworks, and he dragged himself off the sofa to walk unsteadily towards the balcony. His fingers were clumsy with the lock, but he managed to tug open the door, gripping the edge of the frame for support. The night air sobered him enough to see clearly, and he watched the fireworks rise high above the rooftops of London; so high, he imagined Daniel might see them from the heavens above.

James stepped onto the narrow concrete balcony and gripped the rail, shivering slightly as the alcohol began to wear off. His eyes fell to the quadrangle below and he thought of his son lying dead on the path, his lifeblood seeping from his body while the police stood by and watched.

While he'd slept on the chair in his living room.

"I'm sorry," he whispered, and began to cry.

James stayed there until the fireworks finished—Daniel had always loved fireworks—and then reached for one of the white plastic chairs sitting nearby. He pushed it against the edge of the balcony and then, with careful balance, stepped onto it.

One more step, he thought.

Just one more step, and he'd be with Daniel.

Three days later, while James Nkosi's body lay in the mortuary awaiting a coroner's autopsy, Irene held onto Ava's hand tightly as they walked through the streets of London from Walworth Road towards the offices of New Scotland Yard. It was snowing, and Ava's feet skidded against the pavement, but she kept up with her mother's strides, unsure of where they were going but too frightened to ask. She wished she had some gloves or a hat to wear, because her extremities were numb with cold, but she was too scared to say anything about that, either.

Her mother was muttering to herself, again, but Ava couldn't make out what she was saying because the words were coming so fast, they rolled into one long stream of consciousness.

They reached the bridge, where the wind rushed down the river from the sea, buffeting against her young body that was clothed in jeans that were too small and a coat that was too thin.

"Are we—are we nearly there?" she dared to ask.

Her mother didn't reply, but kept walking, dragging her along beside her.

Ava kept her head down and raised her other hand to shield her eyes from the snow, which was coming down more heavily now. Eventually, they reached the other side of the bridge, and, another five minutes later, Irene veered down one of the wide boulevards in that part of the city until they came to a tall office building. A revolving sign told her it was the offices of New Scotland Yard.

"Mum—"

"Come on," Irene said.

She made for the glass entrance doors, which glided open automatically.

As they stepped inside, they were met with a blast of hot air from the heating system, and Ava lingered there for as long as she could while her mother scanned the enormous reception foyer. There was a security desk at the front, and banks of turnstiles through which officers or invited guests could scan a card and gain entry. Without it, there was no access to any of the offices beyond, which were spread over a number of floors.

Irene marched towards the enquiry desk, with Ava trotting behind her.

The woman behind the desk, who was still nursing the effects of a three-day hangover, watched her approach with long-suffering disapproval.

"Can I 'elp you?" she asked.

"I want to speak to the Chief Constable," Irene said. "No—the Commissioner."

The receptionist gave her an empty smile. "Do you have an appointment?" she asked, sweetly.

"No. But, my husband and son are both *dead* because of you and your lot," Irene said, voice trembling with unconcealed rage. "I—want—to—speak—to—someone!"

The receptionist pressed the button beneath her desk, although she didn't need to; the security guard was already making his way across the foyer.

"What's going on, Mandy?"

"This lady says she wants to speak to the Commissioner, but she doesn't have an appointment," the woman explained.

"Right then, come on," the security guard said. "If you don't have a legitimate reason to be here, I'll have to ask you both to leave."

"A—a *legitimate* reason?" Irene cried. "My husband *killed* himself, three days ago!"

"I'm sure we're all very sorry," he said, and reached for her arm. "But that isn't a matter for the Commissioner."

"Isn't it? It's because of him, and his cronies, that our son's murder was never properly investigated! If he ran this place the way he should, he'd have officers who did their jobs rather than turning a blind eye!"

"All right, that's enough," he said, and took a firmer grip on her arm before frog-marching her towards the door. "You too," he said to Ava, who watched the exchange with wide eyes.

"Get your hands *off* me!" Irene shouted. "All I want is justice for my son! That's all we ever wanted, if we can't have him back—"

"Take my advice, and go home," the security guard said. "There isn't anythin' for you here, love."

With that, he slung them back outside, out into the cold.

In the end, they didn't go straight home, but instead went to the only place Irene could find peace.

They went to church.

The minister was a decent man, as far as it went, and had spent many hours offering counsel and company to Irene, when the clinicians at the Maudsley Hospital hadn't been able to do either. He'd rallied the community behind their cause, and been a key supporter throughout their fundraising efforts over the past three years. When he heard the news about James Nkosi, he wished he could say he was surprised.

"Irene, Ava, welcome to God's house," Benjamin said, opening his arms wide. "Come in, and warm yourselves."

The church occupied a modern building which had been purpose-built sometime in the early eighties to house a growing congregation of people in that part of town. The eighties and early nineties hadn't always been kind to working people, and especially not to those who were already on the breadline, so the church had become a place where they could gather, sing, and feel less alone.

"Come and sit down. Ava? How about a hot chocolate?"

Her eyes lit up, and he led them through to his office.

Once they were settled on the visitors' couch in his office with a couple of steaming mugs, Benjamin sat beside them and said a prayer.

"Amen," Irene said.

Ava said nothing, and her mother glared at her.

"Amen," she muttered, belatedly.

She sipped the watery hot chocolate while her mother talked and cried, and the minister spoke of God's Plan, and God's Mercy, and said more prayers. They discussed her father's funeral and how to pay for it, and, of course, Daniel's case.

"The solicitor says we don't have enough evidence to go forward with the private prosecution," Irene said, dabbing tears from her eyes. "I think—I think that's what drove James over the edge. It isn't the solicitor's fault; I think he's done all he can. It's the police. They won't hand over any information and, without it, we can't put together a strong enough case. We've already complained to the Police Complaints Authority and they rejected it, without a right of appeal. I don't think there's anything else I can do."

Benjamin patted her hand. "Have you tried the press?" he said. "I can help you, I know a few of them. Maybe it would put pressure on the police to do the right thing."

"James already tried that," Irene said. "He contacted all the papers and none of them were interested—especially since they'd already reported Daniel's murder as if some young drug-dealer had been killed. Nobody has any sympathy for him, and whoever leaked that story to the press did it because they knew that."

Benjamin sighed. "What do you think, Ava?"

Irene was startled, as if just remembering her daughter was there.

"I—um, I don't know."

But she *did* know. She knew exactly what she was going to do; she'd planned it all, as far as she could. Before Daniel died, she'd had childish dreams of becoming a writer, or maybe a doctor. She'd go to university, work hard and make her family proud. Now, she knew a better way to make her mother proud, and perhaps it was the only way to remind Irene that she still had one child left. In less than four years, Ava would be sixteen and could leave school. Instead of staying to study her A-levels and go on to university, she'd enrol in Police College and join the Metropolitan Police. She'd have to work her way up, of course; she didn't expect to be able to walk straight into the Major Crimes team and work alongside DI Lipman or DS Vaughn. But, in time…

All she had was time.

Time, and a heart that yearned for revenge.

CHAPTER 21

London, Present Day

Ava looked across at her mother, who was sitting in the visitor's chair balancing a book of Sudoku on her lap. She looked older than her sixty-five years; time and cares having worn away the bloom to her skin, long ago. But she was still an attractive woman, and had found a modicum of happiness since becoming the minister's wife a few years ago. God and all of his acolytes were her world now.

"You don't have to stay, if you have somewhere else you need to be, Mum."

Irene looked up from her book. "Don't you want the company?"

Ava wasn't sure how to answer that. She loved her mother and wanted to see her, but not while the woman made it painfully clear that she'd rather be anywhere else.

"I only mean that you shouldn't feel obligated to visit."

"You're my daughter," Irene replied.

Ava experienced a flash of anger as she thought of all the times she'd been forgotten, over the years. She remembered all the dinners she'd made, all the cleaning she'd done at the flat they used to live in when Daniel was alive—

Daniel?

"Daniel," she repeated aloud.

Irene dropped her book on the floor, and bent down slowly to pick it up again.

"Who's Daniel?" Ava asked her.

Irene gripped the edge of the book. "Your brother," she whispered.

"Where is he?"

Irene closed her eyes, and wiped away a single tear, marvelling that she still had any left to shed. "He was murdered in 1995."

Ava stared at her.

Murdered?

"And—my father?"

Irene looked down at her hands, and at the new wedding ring on the third finger of her left hand. She sometimes thought of James, in the quiet moments when she was alone, but never spoke of him. It was easier, that way, to move on from the past.

"James committed suicide, four years after your brother died," she said. "On New Year's Eve in 1999."

Ava closed her eyes, and, for some reason, fireworks came to mind.

"It was so long ago," Irene murmured. "But, I suppose, if you've lost your memory, it will all feel very fresh. I'm sorry, love."

Ava wondered why she wasn't crying. Why did she feel this dreadful emptiness, as though her soul had already departed her body?

"I can't remember either of them," she said. "Do you have a picture?"

Irene always carried a picture of Daniel with her. "Here," she said, tugging a small photograph from her purse. "This is Daniel—I'm sorry, I don't have one of your father. I can bring one, next time, if you like."

Ava held the photo in her hands, and looked into the sweet face of a boy who'd be forever young. He had eyes the same shade as her own, and a smile that brought out the same dimple in her cheek. She looked at the image for a long time, before handing it back to her mother for safekeeping.

She didn't remember him.

"He wanted to be a footballer," Irene said, and looked lovingly at the picture, rubbing the pad of her thumb over his cheek.

Then, she put him back in her purse.

Ava rested her head on the pillow, eyes burning as she watched the play of light on the grubby ceiling overhead.

"A gang of racist thugs killed your brother," Irene continued. "They were never prosecuted because the police didn't do what they should have done, at the time. The investigation was a shambles and we—your father and I—we tried to get justice for Daniel, but they were too powerful, back then. Corruption was rife, and I've always believed they had some reason or another to try to cover for those boys who killed him. Probably, to do with drugs money. A lot has changed in thirty years."

Ava continued to look at the ceiling.

"A few years ago, two of the gang died of drug overdoses," Irene said, still gripping the book on her lap. "I heard about it, through the church, and…Lord, I was *glad*."

She looked up, as if to seek divine forgiveness.

"The third member of the gang who killed your brother is in prison," Irene said. "He was the worst of them; Paul Flint, that's his name. He's behind bars so there's some justice in that, I suppose, but he isn't there to pay for what he did to Daniel. He's in there for some drugs offence; I can't remember what, exactly, although you did tell me a while ago."

Did I? Ava wondered.

"You said he's due out, on parole," Irene continued. "That man is going to be out on the streets, selling drugs and killing more people, no doubt, and there's nothing we can do about it."

"When did I say he gets out of prison?"

"It must be…next month, I think."

Ava looked across at her mother, who'd opened a bag of sweets, which she offered to her.

"No, thanks," she said. "Mum?"

"Yes, love?"

"Does God forgive people for bad deeds, if they act with good intentions?"

Irene was surprised. "I thought you didn't believe in God?"

Ava nodded, and closed her eyes again. "That's right," she said. "Now, I remember."

Alex spent half an hour with Naomi, talking to her about the case he was working on and telling her about what was happening in the news or around the city, before pressing a gentle kiss to her hand and bidding her farewell.

"I'll come and see you later this evening," he promised.

He lingered for a moment, watching her face for any reaction, but she continued to sleep.

From there, Alex made his way up to Ava's ward, which was brimming with visitors who'd come to see her fellow in-patients.

"You just missed my mother," she said. "It seems to be rush hour in here."

Alex checked the time on his watch, which read *nine-twenty*. "I only have half an hour," he said. "Then I've got to hot-foot it over to Scotland Yard, in time for a briefing about that case I mentioned."

"Oh, yes," she said. "How's it progressing?"

"Not as well as I'd hope. But let's talk about how *you're* progressing. How's your memory today?"

Ava reached for the glass of water on her bedside table. "A bit better," she said, after taking a long drink. "I remembered a few things."

"Such as?"

"Such as, I don't believe in God," she said.

Alex gave her a quizzical look. "That's—well, that's useful to know," he said. "I wonder what triggered that memory, in particular?"

"My mother is a devout Christian," Ava said. "She's married to the local minister, now."

"Yes, seeing her might have prompted it," he said, and continued to study her face, which was troubled. "Did you talk to her about your father?"

Ava looked away briefly. "Yes, and it seems my instinct was correct," she replied. "My father died years ago."

She didn't elaborate, and he didn't press her.

"I'm sorry," he said.

"It was a long time ago."

"Time is relative," he replied, and she looked across at him. "I know, people say that time is a great healer. I think it can help, but the person has to be willing to *allow* time to heal them. If you hold on to memories, or to sadness, it perpetuates."

Ava wondered if he could read minds, after all. "Everything feels brand new," she whispered. "Whenever I remember something, it's as though it's only just happened."

"The grief for your father must feel very raw."

She swallowed. "It would, if I could remember more about him."

"Now that the memories are starting to come back, you may find they start flooding in," he said. "You can talk to me anytime, if you need a friendly ear. It can be quite overwhelming."

She felt an odd sort of disquiet—as though she didn't deserve such comfort from him, or from anyone. "My mother told me something else, today," she said. "I had a brother, Daniel. He was murdered when he was only a teenager, by a local gang."

Alex was shocked that she'd never mentioned it to him before, but there were many reasons why people chose to keep things private. Perhaps, for Ava, her brother's death was something she hadn't felt ready to discuss.

"Your family suffered a double loss," he said. "Do you remember Daniel?"

She thought of the boy in the picture. "No," she said. "I only remembered his name, today. Mum filled in the rest."

"Perhaps you don't really *want* to remember, if the memories are too painful," Alex said. "When you're feeling stronger, memories of Daniel might come back to you."

"Time heals?" she said, with a smile.

"Sometimes it does," he acknowledged, but, even as he said the words, he thought of his own family.

Sometimes, the wound remained deep in a corner of your heart, bleeding a little every day.

"I could look Daniel up, on the internet," she said. "But I don't know if I'm ready for that."

"I think you should allow your mind to heal at its own pace," he advised her. "As I said before, there's a risk of becoming overwhelmed."

Ava thought of her nightmare, the previous evening. "I dreamed about Naomi," she blurted out.

He leaned forward. "What happened in the dream?"

Tut, tut, a voice whispered, and Ava fidgeted in the bed, resisting the urge to look over her shoulder.

"I saw Naomi lying on the floor, in the room where we were attacked," she said. "Then, there was—the barrel of a gun was pointed at my head—"

She began to breathe more quickly, panic rising in her chest.

"You're safe here," Alex told her softly. "Remember, you're *safe* now. Keep breathing—that's right—breathe in for four counts, and then out for four counts."

She did as he told her, and felt a bit better.

"Did you see Carl Deere in the dream?"

"No," she said. *But I heard him.*

"Do you remember anything else about the room, or about Naomi? You said she was lying face down?"

"He—Carl must have attacked her before he attacked me," she replied. "I remember seeing a timeline drawn on the wall. I guess you must have done that?"

He nodded.

"There was some more writing on the wall" she said. "It had a Latin phrase written along one side."

"*Vindicta servivit frigus*," he said. "It was just a silly idea I had about Carl's motivations. He was an obsessive character who had a particular liking for acrostics. We found that Latin phrase in his prison cell, and he seemed to be ticking people off a list, so it occurred to me that he might have paired his victims' surnames with the first letters of that phrase. It matched up, with the exception of Ian O' Shea, whose first name fitted with the 'I' letters but not his last name, which wouldn't have been in keeping with Carl's methodical mind. As I say, it was just a foolish idea."

Ava thought of the 'I's that were circled in green in the dream she'd had, and looked down at her hands, expecting to find them covered in green ink. Then, she had a violent image of a good-looking, blond-haired man lying on a sofa, covered in blood.

She inhaled sharply.

"Are you okay?" Alex said.

"I—I think I remembered Ian," she said. "I know how he died; Carter told me. I saw him, just then, with his throat slashed."

She turned pale.

"Have some of this," Alex said, and handed her a glass of water. "Remember to keep breathing."

When she looked down, she saw that her hands were covered in blood.

"Argh!"

She dropped the glass, spilling water all over the duvet as she tried to scrub the blood away.

"Ava!" Alex took her frantic hands in each of his own. "It's okay, I'll call a nurse and have the covers changed," he said, a bit startled by her reaction. "You don't need to worry about it."

"I can't get it *off*," she whispered.

"It's only water," he said. "It can't hurt you."

"No, I—" She said nothing further, so he left her briefly to call one of the nurses. While he was gone, Ava studied her hands, but, to her surprise, there was no blood on them, now.

Was she hallucinating?

Alex returned with one of the nurses who clucked her tongue, told her that 'accidents happened' and hauled her out of bed to perform a quick changeover.

"I'm sorry, I have to go," Alex said, after helping her into the visitor's chair. "Are you sure you're okay? You seem a bit shaken."

Ava looked down at her hands, and forced herself to smile.

"I'm fine, now; don't worry. Go and help to find that little boy," she said.

"The sooner we bring Rory home, the better," he agreed. "It takes a particularly dark mind to play with the life of a child, and the longer this goes on, the more volatile they could become."

She understood that, only too well.

CHAPTER 22

"Smythe wants to pay the ransom."

DCI Verrill made this bald statement to the collection of police personnel gathered in the conference room, as well as Gregory and Douglas, who occupied their usual position beside the door—presumably, to make a quick getaway, should the need arise.

"The Chief Constable has already advised him against it," she continued. "Not only because it goes against government protocol, but because we have no assurances that, even if the bitcoin money is paid, Rory Smythe will be returned home. In fact, we have no reassurance that he's still *alive*, which is far more concerning. As soon as monies are exchanged, their incentive to keep Rory safe and well would rapidly evaporate."

Verrill ran a tired hand through her hair, and wished she'd made a detour for coffee. "Smythe's argument is that, since we haven't gone public with this, nobody will be any the wiser about the fact he's deviated from any protocol," she said. "Even then, he's at the point where he doesn't care anymore. He wants his son back, and he doesn't care what it costs him."

There wasn't a person in the room who didn't sympathise.

"As you know, a second communication was received at eight o'clock this morning," she said. "It gives the family until eight this evening to pay the ransom. Smythe has told us that, unless we're able to locate his son by four o'clock this afternoon, he intends to pay."

There was a heavy silence, in which those gathered in the conference room accepted that it was highly unlikely they would be able to meet that self-imposed deadline; there were just too many avenues and too many potential suspects to explore.

All the same, Verrill wasn't prepared to give up yet. "I want an update on last night's surveillance," she snapped.

One of her officers proceeded to reel off a report.

"In other words, nothing happened," she said, with palpable disappointment. "Everyone under surveillance stayed at home, there've been no reports from neighbours about any strange sounds and no unusual visitors, either."

She paused, considering the legal options available to her, and weighed them up against the gravity of the situation.

"We need three emergency search warrants," she said. "Don't give them any warning. I don't care if they all look like model citizens, we need to be absolutely sure neither Stefanie King, Camilla Smythe nor Gordon Jenkins have Rory Smythe squirreled away. There's only one way of being sure, and that's to go in."

She barked out an order to one of her junior staff, who took off from the room at a run.

"That'll be done within the hour," she said to the room at large. "Assuming none of those individuals has Rory, we have some other potential names based on Jonathan Smythe's political connections. Firstly, the climate activists.

We checked out the list he gave us, and at least two of the people on it have form for GBH, assault and affray. They're not all tree-huggers—not by a long shot."

She went on to discuss an immigration gang who, two years ago, had sent a threatening letter to Smythe's office following his hard-line stance on channel boat crossings, and the Islamic terrorist group who'd included his name in a long list of MPs they planned to target.

"None of those prospects fit the bill," Alex said, not bothering to mince his words.

Verrill happened to agree with him, but she was interested to know if their reasoning was the same. "Oh?" she replied. "Why's that?"

"All three of those target groups thrive on publicity," he said. "There's no conceivable reason why any of them would want to suppress the story from going out in the press, whereas that was a clear instruction in the first ransom note. It doesn't tally."

Her thoughts exactly.

"You may be right, but we cover all bases," she said. "Next up, financials. Any progress from the banks?"

One of the team piped up, and told her the data should be forthcoming by noon.

"Noon isn't fast enough. Call them again," she said. "How about the trace on that e-mail address?"

A gangly, bespectacled young man who looked no older than Smythe's teenage son stood up from his chair and delivered a brief report. Alex listened and reflected that, though it was always dangerous to stereotype people, who were all gloriously individual…sometimes, you couldn't help it, especially when it came to the type of person he might have imagined working in the Digital Forensics department.

"I don't need chapter and verse," Verrill cut him off. "Just tell me whether you've found the bastard or not."

"Er…*not*, ma'am," the young man replied.

"Then, bugger off, and get back to it!"

Verrill's management style wasn't exactly *textbook*, Alex thought, as he watched the aforementioned gangly youth scuttle from the room. On the other hand, she seemed to have a good rapport with her staff in general, so perhaps they were happy to forgive an occasional deviation from the Human Resources Handbook.

"More CCTV footage has come in since yesterday," she continued. "Still no sighting of Rory, but we've got a partial sighting of Camilla Smythe making her way along the high street on her way home from her Pilates class, at around seven-twenty. We have a later sighting of her further up the high street, in the opposite direction from the Smythe residence, a few minutes later. It's possible she could have doubled back but, on the face of it, the footage confirms her version of events."

"What about cars in the area?" Alex asked.

"Too numerous to narrow down, and we have no footage covering the side alley behind the Smythe residence," she said. "One interesting point to note is that their neighbour's camera was vandalised recently, which is a real coincidence, because it means there was no footage in that part of the alleyway leading from the garden gate—which is how we presume Rory left the premises."

It was becoming clear to all of them that the kidnap had been planned in detail, even down to mapping out where CCTV cameras were placed, and making sure they were destroyed ahead of time.

Which was another inconsistency, Gregory thought.

If the kidnappers were new to the game, as their ransom notes suggested, how had they managed to prepare so well? It took patience and time to follow a family's habits, and come to know when Rory would be vulnerable. It took even more time to get to know the streets and cameras around that family's house, and work out the best way to collect Rory without being seen. Every instinct told him it could only have been achieved by someone who was already familiar with those routines, and already familiar with the geographic area. But, if the three most obvious suspects—their housekeeper, their driver and Jonathan's ex-wife—appeared not to have been involved, who did that leave?

"Have you checked Jonathan Smythe's financial situation?" he said.

DCI Verrill appreciated a cynic, being one herself. "You think the father might have had something to do with his own son's disappearance?"

"I think we have to cover all bases, like you said."

She smiled. "I agree, which is why I've ordered a deep dive on Smythe's personal accounts."

If he'd had a glass in his hand, he would have toasted her with it.

Carter intercepted Gregory and Douglas as they left the briefing.

"Do you have a minute?"

"We're on our way over to the Smythe's house, but we can spare ten minutes," Bill said.

"In that case, let's walk and talk," Carter said. "I wanted to ask how Ava's getting on?" He pressed a button for the lifts, and waited.

"Memories are starting to come back to her, now," Alex told him. "She's remembering a lot more about her family and childhood, which I'm sure you already know about."

Carter neither confirmed, nor denied.

"She's had a couple of flashback memories concerning the attack—"

"Such as?"

"It's nothing we don't already know," Alex said. "She saw Naomi, on the ground, and the barrel of a gun. She remembered Ian O'Shea's body, which must have been traumatic."

"Yes, it probably was."

"Hopefully, it won't be long before her long-term memories come back to her, fully," Alex said. "I can't say how long it will take for memories of the attack to come back, because that's more to do with post-traumatic stress, but the fact that she's had a couple of flashbacks would suggest it's closer to the surface than before. I can help her to work on that."

The three men stepped out of the lift and into the reception foyer.

"Ava's had a lot of trauma to contend with, in her life," Alex said. "The more I speak with her, the more I think she isn't suffering from retrograde amnesia, at all. I think she has post-traumatic amnesia surrounding *all* of her lost memories, not just those immediately prior to and during the recent attack."

Carter put a hand on his arm. "That would be good news, wouldn't it?" he said. "If she can work through the PTSD, then there's more of a chance she'd remember everything, right?"

"It's a lot easier," Bill put in. "There are no easy solutions to memory loss, but some are easier than others."

"If I'm right, and it's the PTSD blocking her memories, then Ava has to *want* to remember," Alex said. "The mind blocks things out as a defence mechanism and, sometimes, memories are completely lost during the process, never to be recalled. In this case, well established memories could come back, but not newer, less established memories, or those she has no interest in remembering."

Such as when she'd murdered people, Carter thought.

"Her mobility is much better, too," Alex said, as a parting note. "I don't think she'll need a walking aid, after another week or two."

Carter watched them exit the turnstiles before disappearing into the morning sunshine. Then, he reached for the burner mobile in his inner breast pocket and made an urgent appointment with his contact in Ghost Squad.

CHAPTER 23

Xavier House, 2008

Police Constable Ava Hope parked her car in one of the side streets next to Xavier House, and walked through the pedestrian tunnel towards the quadrangle where her brother had died, thirteen years earlier. After her father passed, she and her mother had stayed on at the flat for a couple of years, until the local minister, Benjamin Hope, had plucked up the courage to ask her mother to marry him. Ava left for Police College shortly after their wedding and, since her mother had taken her new husband's surname, she'd chosen to do the same and had completed the necessary paperwork. It was a happy coincidence that, in doing so, she would avoid any obvious associations with her brother's death while she was at the Met, and would be free to work her way through the ranks without anybody asking awkward questions about her motivations in doing so. Especially not DI Lipman, whose team she planned to join, as soon as an opening came up.

For now, she planned to do what hadn't been done thirteen years ago.

She would *investigate*.

Her footsteps slowed as she came through the tunnel and faced the building she'd lived in for most of her life, so familiar and yet so alien to her, after five years spent away. She'd avoided coming back, not wanting to remember the pathway with its bloodstained tarmac that hadn't worn off for months, or the cold flat where she'd lived such a lonely childhood.

But now, she had a reason to return.

She set off for the entrance to her old block and pushed the buzzer for a flat on the third floor which, according to her research, was still occupied by a man named Vincent Ingleby. It took several attempts but, after the sixth ring, he answered.

"Who is it?"

She spoke up, remembering that he'd be in his mid-eighties, by now. "Mr Ingleby? This is Police Constable Hope, from the Metropolitan Police. May I come up and speak to you, please?"

There was a long pause and, sensing he'd gone to look over the balcony and check she was telling the truth, Ava turned and waved at him.

"All right," he said, a moment later. "Come up."

The door opened, and she made her way along the soulless corridors until she reached Flat 33, where Ingleby waited for her with the door ajar.

"Let's see your warrant card," he said.

Ava produced it, and he held it close to his eyes, which were riddled with cataracts.

He handed it back to her and ushered her inside.

The flat smelled of...well, it smelled of *old people*, Ava thought. A combination of camomile lotion, cottage pie and bodily fluids that had seeped into the ancient carpet and permeated the walls. The addition of three cats—that she counted—didn't help matters, and she sneezed loudly upon entering the living room.

"Are you here about the mugging?" he asked, after she'd perched herself on the extreme edge of his couch. "I heard about it from Gloria, next door. Terrible, what happened to her, although nothing surprises me now."

Ava wondered what horrors his neighbour had been through, but told herself not to deviate from the task in hand.

"Actually, Mr Ingleby, I'm here about an old case," she said. "Do you remember the murder of Daniel Nkosi? He used to live in the building."

His eyes might have been tired, but his mind was still sharp as a tack. "I'll never forget it," he said. "Nice lad, he was, and came from a nice family. He used to stop and help me with my shopping."

Ava bore down against the grief that swept through her body as she remembered how kind Daniel had been. "We're—um—we're going over some cold cases, back at The Yard," she lied. "The Nkosi case is one of them. I was looking over the file and there were a number of potential witnesses whose statements were missing, including yours—"

"*Ay?*" he said, and scratched his head, causing a small snowstorm of dandruff to fall onto his shoulders. "I gave my statement to the police, at the time. In fact, I saw it all happen. Never could understand why they didn't ask me to go to court or nothin'."

Ava's eyes burned. "You—you witnessed the murder?"

He nodded, and began petting one of the cats that jumped onto his lap. "I 'eard 'em, before I saw 'em," he said. "Three of 'em, gruntin' and laughin'. I went outside, onto the balcony, to tell 'em to pack it in. When I saw what was goin' on, I shouted at them to clear off, then I came back in and rang for the police and the ambulance. I didn't know it was Daniel who'd been 'urt, but I knew *someone'd* be in a bad way after the way they'd been goin' at it."

Ava knew the details of her brother's death, but hearing it from someone who'd seen it happen in real time somehow made it all the worse.

"Any'ow, I went down there, to see if 'e was all right, y' know?" Ingleby shook his head, and sniffed. "Poor lad was in a bad way," he said softly. "There weren't nothin' any of us could do except wait for the ambulance, but it was them two police officers that came first, not the paramedics."

"DS Vaughn and DI Lipman?" she said.

"Nah, it was one of 'em and a constable, to begin with," he said. "The other one—the senior one—came along a bit later."

Ava nodded, and made a mental note to check the file again to see which constable had been on duty that night. Perhaps, just *perhaps*, they might have something to tell her.

"I told 'em, straight off, what I'd seen," Ingleby continued. "Especially the lad with the scar. I said I'd seen 'im round and about the place before—proper little toe-rag, he was."

She smiled thinly. "Would you recognise him, after all this time?"

He blew out a long breath, and scratched his head again. "I dunno, love," he said. "If you'd asked me, back then…"

She took a photograph from a folder she carried beneath her arm, and held it out for him to study.

Ingleby clutched it between his arthritic fingers and nodded. "That's him," he said, tapping the image of Paul Flint taken a few years earlier.

"He'd be older, now," she said. "But the image you're looking at was taken around the time Daniel Nkosi died."

"I'm sure that was 'im," Ingleby said, and sniffed loudly. "I remember the police askin' if I'd got a good look, with it bein' dark at the time, but the light was shinin' from the entrance, y' see? It was like a bleedin' spotlight, weren't it?"

"And nobody ever took your statement, formally, or followed up with you?"

"No," he said, and was obviously still baffled about it. "I thought they must've 'ad enough witnesses, or somethin'. I never 'eard from anyone, after."

She thought of all the times her father had spoken of police incompetence and corruption, and wondered which one had been responsible for such a fatal mistake.

"I told Daniel's dad—James, was 'is name—I told 'im I'd seen what 'appened. He complained about it to the coppers, but they done nothin' about it."

He tutted, and continued to stroke the cat, causing layers of fur to rise up on the stuffy air.

"The man tried," he repeated. "But it broke 'im in the end. Went and threw 'imself off the balcony, didn't 'e?"

Ava said nothing, but looked out of the window as she thought of the fireworks that had sounded in the sky the night her father had fallen.

"Would you be willing to make a statement now, Mr Ingleby?"

"Happy to," he said. "But I warn you, love, they wouldn't believe it. I'm eighty-six, and nearly blind. Nobody believes an old duffer like me, do they?"

"I believe you," she said quietly. "I believe everything you've told me."

CHAPTER 24

London, 2016

Eight years later

"Look, sweetheart, there's two ways we can play this: *my* way, or *no* way. D'you understand?"

The newly promoted Detective Constable Ava Hope looked across at her boss, whose sagging profile was silhouetted against the passing lights of the Old Kent Road. After four years on the detective training pathway, during which time she'd fielded any number of inappropriate offers, sly innuendos and racist bigotry, she'd finally secured a transfer onto DI Lipman's team. Now in his early fifties, his face bore the evidence of years of excessive drug and alcohol abuse, and his hands trembled slightly at the wheel of the car.

"I understand," she said, and hated him with every fibre of her being. "So, what's the job?"

"Some bird has been found battered in an alleyway off Camberwell Green and she's sayin' it was rape," he said, with breathtaking callousness. "Take my word for it, these girls are all the same. They tart themselves up on Friday nights, have it all hanging out to find themselves a man, then they come cryin' to us when it all goes tits up. What do they expect, eh? They're not gonna find Prince Charming round the back of a kebab shop in South London."

It made her sick to do it, but Ava played along because she needed to gain his trust.

"Yeah, they bring it on themselves, really."

"That's what I'm *tellin'* you," Lipman said, and jabbed an accusatory finger while he drove dangerously fast through a pedestrian zone. "Now, before we go and deal with all that, I've got a bit of business to attend to. Now—Hope, wasn't it?"

"Yes, sir."

"Remember what I said to you, before. To survive in this game, you've gotta understand how to play it right. Everybody has a little side hustle and that's the way it's always been. You learn to play your cards right, and I'll even think about letting you in on it."

"Thank you, sir."

He nodded, and made a sharp left along one of the residential streets in Camberwell, not far from Xavier House. Presently, he swung into a parking space outside a row of terraced houses, and turned off the engine. He reached across her legs to the glove compartment on the passenger side, and she tried not to shudder as his hand deliberately brushed her thigh as he retrieved a bag of cocaine and a stolen firearm. He wet his fingers and dipped them into the bag, then proceeded to rub the powder over his gums.

Catching her looking at him, he offered the bag. "Need a pick me up? It's a great aphrodisiac," he winked.

Ava thought she might throw up, but managed to affect a lazy smile. "I'm still ridin' from the last hit," she said. "Thanks, though."

He nodded, and shoved the bag back inside the glove compartment. "Stay here," he instructed her.

"I can help?" she offered.

Lipman shrugged. "Might as well learn on the job," he said. "C'mon then."

He slammed out of the car, and Ava followed him to the front door of one of the houses. Outside, the tiny front garden was littered with rubbish and scrap furniture.

The door opened after Lipman leaned on the bell for a while, and Ava came face-to-face with a man she'd never met, but had come to hate over the past seventeen years.

"Wasn't expectin' you today," Paul Flint said to Lipman, before raking a lascivious eye over Ava's body. "Who's your little friend?"

"Fresh meat," Lipman said, with a glint in his eye. "DC Hope, meet Paul Flint, a business associate of mine."

Ava stared at the man who'd killed her brother, and imagined driving a knife into his heart.

"Pleased to meet you," she said.

"You're not due a payment till the end of the month," he said, turning back to Lipman.

"Well, now, I'm not so sure about that. See, me and Vaughn, we happened to notice the last envelope you gave us was a bit *light*." Lipman continued to talk in the same, cheerful tone. "Now, DS Vaughn, he's not as forgiving as me," he said. "He thinks that was deliberate, but I told him it must have been an oversight. I told him, 'You know our old mate Flinty. He'd never try to do a stupid thing like that'."

By then, a couple of other men had joined Flint in the narrow hallway. They were topless, dressed only in baggy jogging pants, and looked as though they'd been sampling their own wares.

"Everythin' aiight?" one of them asked.

"Nothin' to worry about, boys," Flint replied, not taking his eyes from Lipman's face. "We're just havin' a little chat."

"About breach of contract," Lipman said, with a tight smile.

"Yer, well, the terms are changin'," Flint replied.

"Now, look, you little *scrote*—"

It happened very fast, Ava would later think. Lipman moved, as if to reach for the gun in his pocket, but Flint was faster. He had a firearm tucked down the back of his pants, and had it in his hand within seconds. Ava reacted like lightning, knocking it away with one strong swipe, sending it clattering to the floor. While they scrambled for it, she grabbed Lipman's arm, and together they legged it back to the car. Once he'd fired up the engine and accelerated down the street, he turned to her.

"That was fast thinking back there, Hope."

"Thank you, sir."

"Thank *you*," he said, and patted her leg with one beefy hand. "It looks like you're going to be very useful to have around."

She swallowed bile, and put her hand over his.

"Are you doing anything later?" she said. "You could…teach me a few more things, round at your place."

Lipman grinned to himself.

Women, he thought. *They were all alike.*

Lipman lived in a modern, two-bedroom flat in a new development on the Isle of Dogs, near Canary Wharf. It was, in Ava's opinion, a soulless part of London, thriving with financiers during the weekdays but almost deserted at weekends, and starved of anything resembling a community.

Which suited her new boss perfectly.

Her stomach trembled as they approached his apartment building, and her hand strayed to her jacket pocket, checking for the third or fourth time that it contained the syringes she'd put there at the start of the day.

Lipman looked back at her as he opened the outer door. "Welcome to Casa del Lipman."

There was no CCTV in the entrance foyer, she was pleased to find, and didn't need to ask why that might be. If he had various business dealings on the go, it was likely he'd come to some arrangement with the building's security team to ensure none of his adventures were captured on film.

Perfect, she thought.

He unlocked the door to his flat, and gestured for her to precede him. "After you," he said, playing the gentleman.

Ava stepped inside and had barely any time to think of her next move before his arms came around her, pawing at her body while his lips sought hers.

There was a very real risk she would vomit, and she took evasive measures. "Let me just go to the bathroom," she said, coquettishly. "I want to freshen up."

"You're fresh enough," he muttered, making a grab for her chest.

She giggled, and gave him a playful shove. "Why don't you open a bottle of wine?"

He decided that he could be patient for a few more minutes. She was a good-looking one, he thought, and considerably younger than he was, which was always a bonus. He didn't question her attraction for him, because women loved a powerful man like him, didn't they?

They couldn't get enough of it.

Ava locked the bathroom door and leaned back against it, breathing hard through her teeth before retching into the sink as quietly as she could. She'd never been more repulsed by another person, and it was only the thought of her brother that sustained her.

"You can do this," she whispered to her reflection in the bathroom mirror. "This is the opportunity you've been waiting for."

She pulled out the firearm she'd lifted from his glove compartment and tested its weight in her hand.

"Now or never," she whispered.

"Take off your belt."

Lipman set two wine glasses on the rickety coffee table in his living room, and raised his eyebrows.

"I like a woman who doesn't mess about," he said, and began undoing his belt. "I get it. You want to be in charge, just for tonight, eh? I don't usually go in for that, love, but there's a first time for everything."

Ava smiled. "Put the belt on the table," she said softly. "Now, take off your shirt."

He gave her a look that turned her stomach again. "You gonna do the same?"

"All in good time," she said.

He took off his shirt, revealing an enormous beer belly covered in wiry grey hair.

"Mm," she purred. "I like a man I can grab onto. Now, sit back on the sofa."

He did as she asked, and spread his legs wide, an expectant grin on his face.

"Hop on, love."

Ava took a pair of nitrile gloves from her pocket, and pulled them on. Then, she retrieved a couple of pre-filled syringes and set them on the coffee table beside the wine glasses. He watched, and blew out a long breath.

"I dunno if I can manage any more, tonight," he said. "I've had a bit of snow today and I'm already hopping from it."

"Aww," she said, and removed her jacket while he watched. "Don't be a spoilsport."

She moved closer, and came to sit on the edge of the coffee table, between his legs.

"Besides," she whispered, reaching for the firearm she'd tucked down the back of her trousers. "I'm not really giving you a choice, Detective Inspector."

Lipman found himself looking at the business end of his own illegal firearm. "What the—"

"Ah-ah," she said, and nudged him back against the sofa. "Don't make any sudden moves, or I might pull this trigger, accidentally."

His face darkened. "What's happening here?" he growled.

"*Justice*," she said. "Now, hold out your hand."

When he didn't comply, she pointed the gun at his genitals. "Do as I say."

Lipman held out a trembling hand, and she reached behind her for the belt he'd discarded, which she placed into his palm. Then, watching him carefully, she stood up and moved a few feet away, still aiming the gun at his head.

"Tie your belt around your arm," she instructed him.

"Bugger off."

She took a step closer, and something in her eyes must have frightened him, because he made a grab for the belt. "Is this all part of some kink you've got?" he said, with a nervous laugh. "You get off on the fear?"

"Tie the belt tighter."

He did as he was told, and she waited until she could see the veins pumping in his arm.

"One of those syringes contains heroin," she said. "The other one has been mixed with poison."

He looked at the syringes sitting on the coffee table. "You're—you're joking."

"Do I look like I'm joking?"

He looked into her eyes and an old memory stirred. "I—I know you from somewhere."

She smiled.

"Yes, you do. You protected my brother's murderers for your own financial gain. You failed to investigate, and spread lies about him being a drug dealer. You treated my family like dirt, and drove my father to despair. You, along with DS Vaughn, Paul Flint and his little gang, destroyed my family and now it's time to pay for it."

"Nkosi," he said after a second's pause. "You're Ava Nkosi."

She gestured with the gun. "Are you going to choose, or do you want me to choose for you?"

"Look," he said. "I understand you think you know something, but you're wrong—"

"No, I don't think I am," she replied, in the same maddeningly calm tone. "I saw how pally you were with Flint, earlier this evening, remember? Well, at least until he tried to shoot you, but I guess all business partners have their little disagreements."

"You'll never get away with this."

"With what? I'm giving you a fifty-fifty chance, which is more than my brother was given," she said. "Now, make your choice, or I'll inject you with the syringe containing poison—remember, I know which one it is."

To his everlasting shame, Lipman wet himself.

"That's embarrassing," she said, and took another step forward. "Get on with it."

He could overpower her, Lipman thought.

But he'd never make it past the gun, and her trigger finger would always be faster than he was.

"You're bluffing," he said, and hoped it was true. "You'd never get away with this. You just want to give me a scare."

"Play along, then," she snarled. "You know what to do—it isn't as if you haven't shot up before, Detective."

He studied her face, and then let out a laugh that was all bravado.

"You'd never use that thing," he said, jutting his chin towards the gun she held. "You wouldn't know how."

She aimed the gun squarely at his head.

"Well, you know, even if I hadn't graduated top of my class in firearms training, the great thing about being at this sort of close range is that the chances of missing you are vastly reduced," she said, conversationally. "I don't *have* to know much about firing this gun. I only have to point it at your head or your chest, and pull the trigger."

She smiled, grimly.

"I'm a fair woman, Detective. I've given you the choice of two syringes, so your fate is in the lap of the Gods. Do you feel lucky?"

He began to cry; great, snivelling tears that ran down his cheeks.

"I'm sorry, all right? I'm sorry about your brother. Is that what you want? You want me to beg, too? I'll beg, I'll get on my knees—"

Ava could stand no more of it and, before he had time to react, she'd crossed the distance between them and snatched up the closest syringe to hand. In seconds, she'd plunged it into his arm, and he could only look at her, his mouth forming a shocked 'o'.

His body sank back against the sofa and began to convulse.

"I have another confession to make," she said quietly, as she watched him die. "Both of the syringes contained poison."

After it was done, she looked at him for long minutes, waiting for the guilt to come, but it never did. She felt nothing; no elation, no emotion, *nothing*.

Ava spent some time cleaning and tidying away the extra wine glass, and staging the living space so that Lipman would appear to have been on his own in the flat. She left the belt hanging from his arm along with the syringe, and then removed the additional syringe which she capped and put back in her pocket. Finally, she cleaned the edge of the sink in the bathroom as well as the door handle and anything else she might have touched. She kept the gun in her pocket, deciding to save it for the next time she might need it.

One down, she thought. *Four to go.*

CHAPTER 25

London, Present Day

Gregory and Douglas made their way to the Smythe's home in Greenwich, where they found Rory's parents in turmoil.

"I won't wait any longer," Jonathan told them. "So, if you've come to try to convince me not to pay the ransom, you've had a wasted journey. I'll *pay* whatever they ask and I'll *do* whatever they ask, because I want my son back. It's been almost two days, and he might already be—be—"

He couldn't bring himself to say 'dead'.

"We're not here to convince you of anything," Bill said, in a tone he might have used to calm one of his former patients. "We're here because we don't think you've been completely honest with us."

"What are you insinuating?" Anita said, looking between them and her husband.

"Why aren't there more pictures of Theo around the house?" Alex countered. "In every room of this house, there are beautiful, framed images of you and Rory. You told us Theo is a good brother, a good son, and that you all get along. If that's true, why isn't he included? Where are Theo's pictures?"

Jonathan and Anita exchanged a look.

"Why has your ex-wife paid so many visits to the house, lately? What was it she needed to discuss with you, about Theo?" Alex continued. "These are valid questions, and we need answers."

Jonathan rubbed a hand over his mouth, and nodded. "Yes—yes, alright. I'm sorry, I—I should have told you earlier, but I can't see how it's relevant. Theo had a drugs problem for a couple of years, and was expelled from his last school. It put a big strain on his relationship with us, and with his mother, too. We may have our differences, but Camilla and I both care for Theo and wanted him to get well again."

"He spent some time at The Priory," Anita said quietly. "He came through the rehab program really well, and it was like having the old Theo back again."

Jonathan nodded. "I got my son back," he said. "He'd been so difficult to deal with, as you can imagine. It wasn't just the drugs, it was everything else that surrounds it. Given my position, we tried to keep things as private as possible, which is why I didn't want to mention this, at first—for Theo's sake, as well as mine and that of the Party. The papers love nothing better than to drag prominent people, and their families, through the mud. He's still a child, in many ways."

"Where is Theo now?" Alex asked him.

"At his mother's house."

"Would you mind asking him to come round, for a chat?" Alex said.

"You can't think Theo's involved!" Jonathan blustered. "He was with us here, the whole evening. He might have made some mistakes, but that certainly doesn't make him a kidnapper. I know my son, Doctor. He wouldn't do this."

Alex said nothing, and Smythe pulled out his mobile.

"Fine," he said. "I'll call him, now, and you can ask him yourself."

They waited, but there was no answer from Theo.

"Probably let his battery run down again," Smythe muttered, and brought up Camilla's number instead.

After a couple of rings, his call was answered.

"Camilla? It's me. Yes, we're coping as well as you could expect…look, I need to speak to Theo. He's not answering his phone. Could you put him on the line, please?"

His brows drew together in a frown.

"I don't understand this. Theo told me he was going to see you—right, yes. Okay. Please let me know if you see him, Camilla. All right, bye."

Smythe looked at the phone in his hand, then at the others in the room. "Theo isn't at Camilla's house," he said, softly. "She hasn't seen or heard from him, at all."

"I'll check upstairs, just in case he came back," Anita murmured, and left the room at a run.

"We need a list of Theo's friends," Bill said. "Who does he spend the most time with?"

Smythe looked as though he'd aged ten years in the space of ten minutes. "He—he doesn't have too many friends left, after what happened," he said. "He had a girlfriend for a while, but they broke up recently."

"What's her name?" Alex said.

"Daisy Richmond," he replied. "She's actually the daughter of one of the shadow ministers, which was another sore point between us. I'm sure he was only interested in her because he knew the connection would be awkward for me."

"How did they meet?"

"When we reconciled, I brought him along to a charity event with me," Smythe said. "Daisy was there, and they hit it off. She's a year older, but they seemed to get along until lately."

Gregory and Douglas thought privately that the timing of the supposed break-up could be significant, but they said nothing of that.

"He's not upstairs," Anita whispered, as she shuffled back into the room.

"I can't take this in," Smythe was saying, mostly to himself. "Theo *wouldn't* hurt Rory. I won't believe it."

But he thought of how much Rory idolised his elder brother, trailing after him like a puppy.

He'd have done whatever Theo asked of him.

"Does Daisy live with her parents? What's their address?" Bill asked him.

"She—no, they bought her a flat recently," Smythe said. "I don't know the address, but I can find out."

While Anita dabbed fresh tears from her eyes, he brought out his phone again, this time to put a call through to his aide.

"Henry? I need you to find an address for me, urgently," he said, and gave the details. "Yes, I know…just tell them Theo is missing and we're looking for him. That should be reason enough."

He looked around the room, at the photographs Gregory had mentioned. "Theo would do this to us, because we don't have more pictures on the wall?" he murmured.

Alex shook his head. "No, not because of that."

Smythe rubbed a hand over his eyes. "*Why*, then?"

"To punish you," Bill said. "Both of you."

Anita thought of when she'd first met Theo, as a nanny and general au pair. She'd dropped him at school, and they'd watched movies together. She hadn't planned to fall in love with his father, but she understood why Theo might have seen her as the classic 'homewrecker' who'd been responsible for breaking up his family. He wasn't to know that the relationship between Camilla and Jonathan was already strained, nor that they slept in separate bedrooms and had done so for a while before she'd ever come into their lives. Still, after all the years she'd spent building bridges and helping him to conquer his addiction to marijuana and cocaine, she really thought they'd become friends.

As for Rory…

"I thought Theo loved him," she said. "He's always been so kind to Rory."

"Appearances can be deceptive," Bill said. "Especially if the plan was to build his trust."

"You're talking as if he's already been tried and found guilty!" Smythe said. "I, for one, want to give Theo the benefit of the doubt. I'm sure there's an explanation for why he isn't at his mother's house. As for him wanting to punish us..." He paused, remembering some of the unsavoury things he'd said, in the midst of his drug use. "If there was resentment in the past, he's moved on from it," he said, with slightly less conviction than before.

Alex had a sudden thought. "Mr Smythe, you told us that the CCTV camera outside the back door had been damaged while your son was playing basketball. *Which* son were you referring to?"

Smythe nodded, and held his head in his hands. "Theo," he said. "It was Theo who broke the camera."

CHAPTER 26

Daisy Richmond had been given the best of everything.

As an only child to adoring parents, she'd been spoiled since her very first breath, when her mother and father had gazed down into her lovely face and decided, there and then, that she would conquer the world. She'd also won the genetic lottery, having been blessed with the kind of even, attractive features that met the beauty standards of the age, and a generous helping of intelligence—particularly, when it came to mathematics and computer science. Having aced her final exams at the elite private school she'd attended, Daisy had turned down a place at Cambridge, preferring to remain in London where she could be in the thick of it.

Eager to please, as ever, her parents had stumped up the cash for a garden flat in Blackheath, not far from Greenwich, especially if she covered the distance in the snazzy little Fiat they'd also bought for her. One thing they'd been unable to account for was an undiagnosed personality disorder which had, over the years, led to certain deviant behaviours from their daughter. They'd taken great pains to hush it up—sending her to a series of discreet psychiatrists and paying for a new library, when she'd set part of the school's old one alight, for example—but, as she grew older and more independent, it became increasingly difficult to keep track of their daughter's movements. However, since she achieved the highest grades and was, in all other ways, the model daughter, they told themselves it was just a passing phase and nothing to worry about.

Then, she'd met Theo.

For a while, they'd been inseparable, like two souls who'd been kept apart and were now reunited. There wasn't a single day when Daisy hadn't trotted over to the Smythe's house, or vice versa, and the intensity of their bond had been a worry to both families—not least because they stood for opposing political parties. Theo had only recently finished his rehabilitation program and was trying to complete the first year of his exams at a new school, so he hardly needed any distractions. As for Daisy, she had university to look forward to. When they announced their break-up, their parents had been quietly glad.

However, when Jillian Richmond received an unexpected call from Henry Gardiner to ask for her daughter's address, she knew immediately it would have something to do with Theo, and her heart sank.

Armed with an address, Smythe instructed his driver to take him and Gregory to Blackheath, leaving his wife in the capable hands of Professor Douglas.

"We should wait for the police," Alex said. "DCI Verrill is on her way."

Smythe stepped inside the car, forcing him to follow or be left behind.

"If you're right, and we find Theo there with Rory, I want to hear from my son before anybody else has a chance to speak to him," he said, once they were on the road. "I want to know what I did to make him hate me so much."

Alex watched the passing houses from the passenger window, wondering how to explain to a father the machinations of his seventeen-year-old son who, by his own admission, had felt abandoned and replaced. It was obvious, even to a casual observer, that affection didn't come naturally to a man like Jonathan Smythe, and that could have wide-ranging consequences on children, depending on individual personality type. In Theo's case, he wondered if the drug use had been a cry for attention, but jealousy was an equally strong motivator, and it must have been difficult for the elder boy to watch his younger brother receive all the love and praise that he coveted for himself.

"I don't think he hates you," Alex said. "I think he loves you."

Smythe shook his head. "This is my fault," he said. "I wasn't there for him, as I've been there for Rory."

"That might be true, but there are plenty of parents in the world who aren't able to spend as much time with their children as they'd like to," Alex said. "It doesn't always lead to this."

Smythe nodded, and turned to stare out of the window. "If Theo has done this to Rory, and to us, how can I forgive him?"

Alex didn't have the answer to that.

Five minutes later, they arrived at their destination.

Daisy Richmond's maisonette flat was on the ground and lower-ground floors of an Edwardian house at the end of a long terrace, on a pretty, tree-lined street not far from the heath that gave 'Blackheath' its name. A white Fiat 500 was parked on the kerb outside, but the plantation-style shutters were closed on the bay window at ground floor level.

With Gordon's quiet, hulking presence beside them, they made their way to the front door and rang Daisy's intercom.

No reply.

They tried a second time, then a third, to no avail.

"We could see if there's a back door," Gregory suggested.

As they turned away, the front door opened by a woman who might have been anywhere between the ages of sixty and eighty.

"Are you here to see Daisy?" she asked them.

"Yes, do you know if she's in?"

"I should say so. I've heard plenty of banging and clattering down there today, and the radio's been blasting—that's probably why she didn't hear the buzzer."

"Have you happened to see a young boy come through here over the past few days?" Alex asked. "Around eight years old?"

The woman shook her head. "I thought I heard a child's voice, the other night," she said. "But that was probably just the television."

They thanked her, and made directly for the door to Daisy's flat, which was at the end of the hallway. As they approached, they heard the sound of the radio and, beneath it, something that sounded very much like a young boy's cry.

"That's Rory!" Smythe said.

"Stand aside," Gordon told them, and planted his boot against the wood to give it a couple of hard kicks.

It splintered open, and the three men rushed inside.

Daisy and Theo jumped off the sofa as the door burst from its hinges, but there was no time to run, nor to hide. Gordon entered the room first, scanning the space with an ex-military eye, before pronouncing it clear for Smythe to enter, with Alex bringing up the rear.

Jonathan looked into his son's eyes and knew that his worst fears had been confirmed. Gregory and Douglas were right; the truth of it was written all over his face.

"*Theo*," he said, in a voice that shook.

"What are you doing here, Dad?"

Smythe gave him a long, level look. "I'm going to ask you this once," he said. "And I want you to tell me the truth."

Theo lifted his chin, defiantly.

"Do you know where Rory is?"

"I've already *told* you, I have no idea—"

They heard a soft moan coming from the room next door, which happened to be the spare bedroom. Gregory was nearest, and he hurried across to the door, only to find it locked. He used his shoulder and, with the help of Gordon's bulk, managed to break a second door from its hinges. Inside, they found a spartan room devoid of furniture except for a single bed, a bucket and a large bottle of water.

Rory was curled up on top of the bed, his wrists tied to the brass frame with a thin rope that had dug deep red lines in his skin. He'd been gagged, and seemed to be coming in and out of consciousness.

"*Rory!*" Smythe dashed forward.

"Rory, are you alright? It's Daddy," he whispered. "I'm here."

He turned to Gregory, who was already crossing the room.

"He isn't responding—please—"

He stumbled aside to allow him to examine the boy, which he did with quick, gentle hands.

"He's been given something," Alex muttered. "I'll call the ambulance, but we need to know what they've given him. Hopefully, just a sedative to keep him quiet, but in a child his size any overdose can be fatal."

Gordon remained in the living room to keep a sharp eye on Daisy and Theo, who clung to one another on the sofa.

"What did you give Rory?" he asked. "*Come on*! What was it?"

Their lips remained sealed, so Jonathan cut Rory's hands free and cradled him in his arms while they awaited the paramedics. Theo rose from the sofa and came to stand in the bedroom doorway, watching them both while Gordon put a warning hand on his shoulder.

"I remember, years ago, I fell off my bike," he said. "I was about four, and it was just before Anita came and ruined everything. I hurt my leg, and you lifted me off the ground and held me, just like that." There was a wistful note to his voice, and silent tears began to roll down his young face, which he swatted away with an angry hand. "I didn't want to hurt Rory," he said. "Not really."

Smythe lifted his head. "Just me?"

"Just you," Theo said, and heard the sound of a siren approaching in the street beyond. "Does Anita know about Stefanie, by the way?"

Jonathan closed his eyes, hating himself. "No, she doesn't."

"Lucky for you that I won't be able to tell her," Theo replied. "I guess you hate me now, don't you, Dad?"

Jonathan remembered the day Theo was born, and the joy he'd felt at becoming a father for the first time. He remembered feeding him bottles of milk and reading him stories at bedtime. Before his career had taken off, there'd been time to watch him run races at Sports Day and play frisbee in the park. Life had moved on, the wheel turning faster and faster until, one day, he'd looked up to find Theo was as tall as he was and no longer the little boy he remembered. Then, when he'd got into all that trouble, and been expelled from school, he felt responsible but, at the same time, unable to get through to the child he remembered from long ago. He supposed, when Rory was born, he'd considered it a second chance.

"I don't hate you," he said, almost inaudibly. "I might not have been all I could be, over the years, but I can't forgive you for this, Theo. I would never have believed you capable of something so terrible."

Theo's face twisted into something ugly. "I'm your son, aren't I?" he said. "Everything I am, I learned from you."

CHAPTER 27

London, 2016

A month had passed since Lipman's death, which had been ruled 'accidental' following a massive overdose of heroin mixed with a lethal combination of other chemicals to be found readily in the cleaning aisle at the supermarket. Nobody questioned it, because it was widely known around The Yard that the late Detective Inspector Lipman had been partial to long-term recreational drug use. Since there were no other suspicious circumstances and the last person to have seen him alive, Detective Constable Hope, confirmed that she'd left him in good spirits at the end of their shift and without any reason to be concerned, that had been the end of the matter.

Or so she'd thought.

"DC Hope."

Ava turned to find Detective Sergeant Vaughn standing next to her in the queue at the staff canteen.

"Hello, sergeant."

"The boss says we'll be workin' together a lot more, now that Lipman's gone."

"I'll look forward to it," she said, and meant it. Working with Vaughn was exactly what she'd been angling for, during the past month.

"You know, it's funny," he continued, as they pushed their trays along the line towards the cashier's desk. "I was havin' a chat with a friend of mine, the other day, and d' you know whose name came up? *Yours.*"

"Small world," she said.

His lips curled into a smile.

"The thing is, this friend of mine, he said he'd met you the same night Lipman died," Vaughn continued, keeping his voice low. "He said you were introduced right before there was an unfortunate difference of opinion between him and DI Lipman."

Paul Flint, she realised.

"I don't know who you're talking about."

"Oh, I think you do," Vaughn said, and reached for a plate of shepherd's pie, smiling at the pretty canteen server he'd been working on for months. "What's more, it's funny you never mentioned that visit in your witness statement. You said that you and Lipman went directly to the call out in Camberwell, wrote it up, took statements and then Lipman dropped you off at the tube station at the end of your shift. There was no mention about havin' paid our friend a visit, that night."

Ava thought swiftly. "Did you really *want* me to mention the relationship Lipman had with Paul Flint?" she hissed. "It's obvious you have a similar arrangement, so you should be thanking me for keeping my trap shut." She grabbed a bowl of jelly from the dessert counter, before continuing. "If you must know, Lipman invited me along and said, if I learned the ropes, he'd think about cutting me into whatever deal you've got going. Now that he's gone, that leaves an opening, doesn't it?"

They paid for their meals and then found a quiet table in the canteen area where they wouldn't be disturbed.

"Who says I need a partner?" Vaughn said, once they were seated. "If I work alone, I take home my cut and Lipman's, too."

"And if you work alone, you have nobody to watch your back," she reminded him. "Nobody to give you an alibi when you need it, either."

That was a fair point.

"How do I know I can trust you?"

"You don't, but I could say the same of you," she said, and took a bite of her ham and cheese sandwich. "We'd be in it together, just like you and Lipman were. You scratch my back, and I'll scratch yours."

He watched her face, and wondered why something about her seemed so very familiar.

"Besides," she said. "I've already lied in my statement about what happened the night Lipman died. Why would I risk doing that, if I wasn't prepared to go all in?"

Vaughn shovelled a forkful of shepherd's pie into his mouth. "We could do a trial run," he conceded.

She nodded. "Look, why don't I come round to your place later on and we can talk it over?"

He wiped his mouth with the back of his hand, and pushed his plate away. "No offence, but you're not my type."

She almost laughed. "No offence, Vaughn, but you're not mine, either. What I'm proposing is a strictly business relationship."

He shrugged. "All right then. Come over around eight, and we can talk terms."

Ava smiled, and polished off the rest of her sandwich.

Unlike his former partner, DS Vaughn lived in a squalid, one-bedroom flat in the Finsbury area of North London which looked as though it hadn't been cleaned in several decades. However, Ava wasn't as concerned about his cleanliness as much as she was about his security arrangements, and the degree to which she risked being seen entering his building by a nosy neighbour. Luckily, the other tenants in his building seemed to be students, judging by the stream of grungy-looking youths heading in and out of the main doors, and, in her jeans and overcoat, she kept her head down and moved past them to the first floor.

Vaughn answered on the fourth knock.

"You took your time," she said, and stepped inside. "Thought you might want a beer."

She held up a six-pack, and he grunted—the closest thing to a 'thank you', in Vaughn's world.

"Where's the fridge?"

He let the door slam shut and led her through a dingy hallway towards a tiny galley kitchen.

"Here," she said, handing them over to him. "Might as well have 'em nice and cold."

"Yeah," he agreed, and shoved them in beside a block of mouldy cheese and a couple of microwave curries.

He straightened up again, and turned to find her looking at him strangely.

"What?" he asked, belligerently.

Something about her eyes gave him the creeps, he thought.

Then, he looked down, and saw what she was holding in her hand.

"Don't do anything stupid," she said quietly. "I want you to sit on the floor."

"You stupid b—"

"Now, now," she said, calmly. "Don't say anything you might regret. Do as I tell you, and sit on the floor."

He swore at her, and made a lunge for one of the sharp knives in a block on the counter, but she slammed the butt of Lipman's stolen firearm down against his wrist so that he cried out in pain and fell back.

"*Sit*," she ordered.

Vaughn slid down to the floor. "Is this your way of negotiating better terms?" he asked. "You could've just asked."

Ava smiled, and crouched down so they were face-to-face while she continued to point the weapon at his chest.

"I should come clean and tell you that I really have no intention of going into business with you, sergeant. In fact, your business enterprise is going to be coming to an abrupt end, very soon."

"You're gonna grass me up?" he said, with a laugh. "You've got no idea who you're messin' with."

"I've come to know a lot about you, over the years," she said. "I've watched your comings and goings, I've spoken to some of the victims you never helped, and the families of those victims you ignored and lied to. I know about the relationship with Paul Flint, and where you've put all that money—although, it isn't hard to guess, considering your nose looks as though it could collapse any day now."

He let out a stream of filthy language, which she ignored.

"Now, I'm a fair woman," she said, reaching inside her jacket pocket. "I'm going to give you a choice, and the odds are fifty-fifty in your favour."

She set out two syringes on the linoleum floor and rolled them towards him.

"What d'you expect me to do with those?"

"Choose one, and stick it in your arm," she said, cheerfully. "One contains pure heroin, while the other has been mixed with a few other things that are even less healthy. Now, do you need a tourniquet? You're quite a bit skinner than Lipman was, so I'm guessing you'll be fine without."

He stared at her with dawning comprehension.

"Why—why are you doing this?"

"Can't you guess?"

The eyes, he thought again. *He'd seen those eyes before.*

"Nkosi. Sweet Jesus. You're Daniel Nkosi's sister."

"Full marks," she said. "And I have to congratulate you on having an excellent memory, especially after all the abuse you've put your body through, these past few years. I'm surprised you even remember your own name, half the time."

"What's this about, then?" he said. "You want me to say 'sorry'?"

"No," she said. "I just want you to pick a syringe."

"Forget it."

"Pick one, or I'll do it for you."

"You can try," he said.

Ava was caught off guard for a second as he lunged forward, coming at her with wild, angry eyes. He managed to grab the barrel of the gun, but she didn't hesitate.

She pulled the trigger.

Vaughn's body jerked violently, and he coughed a small spray of blood in her face.

She pulled the trigger a second time, just to be sure, and he fell back on the kitchen floor with a thud, his body twitching as the front of his t-shirt began to turn a deep, burgundy red.

"Are you sorry now?" she wondered.

His eyes stared up at her, while he began to make choking sounds deep in his throat.

It wouldn't be long now.

Quickly, she retrieved the syringes from the floor, and hopped out of the way as a puddle of blood edged towards her. Downstairs, the music had stopped, presumably because someone had heard the gunshots. She stood there, waiting for the inevitable knock at the door, but then the music ramped up again.

"That's the problem with living in a city," she said to Vaughn's body. "Nobody cares about their neighbours."

Ava gave it another ten minutes, then retrieved the six-pack from the fridge and let herself out of the flat using a fresh pair of nitrile gloves, choosing her moment to slip out of the front door while the crowd downstairs was occupied. She walked swiftly down the road, not stopping until she reached her car, which was parked on another street. The firearm burned a hole in her pocket, and she knew she would have to find a way to get rid of it, but not yet.

There were three more to go.

She sat behind the wheel of her car and waited again for the guilt to come.

But it never did.

All she felt was vindication, and a deep sense of peace she hadn't known in years.

She'd have to be careful, or killing could become a habit.

London, 2019

Three years after Vaughn's death

"Detective Inspector Hope, meet your new sergeant, Ben Carter."

Ava looked up from an inspection of some telephone records to find DCS Campbell standing beside her desk, with a man she'd never seen before.

"Pleased to meet you," Carter said, and held out a hand. "I've heard a lot of good things."

She snorted, but took his hand. "Where've you come from, Carter?"

"Thames Valley," he said. "I'm hoping to see a bit more action in the big city."

"You mean to say there's not much happening around Oxfordshire, aside from stolen bikes and drunk students?"

"Don't forget the vandalism," he said, with a grin.

"Well, I can see you two are going to get along," Campbell said, and left them to it.

"D' you need a tour of the office? An ergonomic chair?" she offered.

Carter shook his head.

"I just need to know where the vending machine is," he said.

"A man after my own heart," Ava said. "This way."

They made small talk, as she led him along the corridor towards the chocolate dispenser.

"It's been a while since I had a new sergeant," she said.

"Yeah, I heard about DS Vaughn," Carter said, slotting a few coins into the machine. "I was sorry to hear it."

"Don't be," she said, and nudged the machine with her hip. "It's a bit sticky," she added.

"I take it, Vaughn wasn't all that popular?"

"You could say that," Ava replied. "He was bent, for one thing."

"I heard he was in bed with one of the gangs," Carter said. "I guess if you play with fire…but, they never found a murder weapon, did they?"

"No, but ballistics analysed the rifling marks on the bullets they recovered from his body," she said. "They were the same as those found at other gang shootings, so we have to assume it was all related."

Because the gun that killed him had been lifted from the evidence store by DI Lipman, she thought.

"I suppose Vaughn got what he deserved."

Ava smiled. "What about you, Carter? Do you have any dirty little secrets you need to get off your chest?"

He began to unwrap a Flake bar.

"I'm an open book," he said, while chocolate drifted down his shirtfront.

"Then we'll get along just fine."

CHAPTER 28

London, Present Day

It was late afternoon by the time Alex Gregory stepped back through the automatic doors of St. Thomas' Hospital, his friend having opted to stay with the Smythe family to offer whatever support he could during the aftermath of what had been the most traumatic event of their lives. On the ferry from Greenwich to the north side of the Thames at Embankment, Alex reflected on the notion of familial loyalty and what he might do, were he to find himself in Jonathan Smythe's shoes. It was a difficult question, made all the more so because he could understand what had driven Theo Smythe to such extreme measures.

Understand, but not condone.

Abandonment was a powerful feeling, one he'd experienced for much of his childhood and, he dared say, some of his adulthood, too. His mother's troubles were well documented, but Alex considered his father equally culpable; he'd left his wife and children to start a new life and, even when two of those children died, he hadn't deigned to come back and claim the last remaining. Instead, he'd abandoned Alex to the system, as though he and his siblings had never existed, obliterating every happy memory they'd ever made together in one fell swoop.

In the case of Theo and Rory Smythe, neither child had been wholly abandoned—not physically, at least—but these things were relative. In Theo's mind, his father left him the moment he had an affair and married another woman, and his feelings were compounded when another child came along, who also happened to be a boy. Jonathan Smythe had asked how to forgive his elder son, and Alex still didn't have an answer to that question. If Theo demonstrated meaningful remorse, forgiveness was always possible, but the more likely scenario was that the family would be estranged. Alex doubted whether the boy felt any remorse; however, time served in one of His Majesty's young offenders institutions could often change even the hardest of hearts.

Alex made his way towards the lifts to see Naomi, but found himself thinking of Ava and of the brother she'd lost years ago. He'd spent some time the previous evening searching for details of 'Daniel Hope' and had found nothing; however, an old news story concerning a boy named 'Daniel Nkosi' had flagged up, along with an old photograph of Ava's mother, Irene. The old articles detailed the brutality of his killing, by unknown gang members, before going on to suggest that, as a young dealer, Daniel had it coming. If you got into bed with people like that, then you could expect to wind up dead on a pathway somewhere, or so the commentators suggested.

Another search of the name 'Nkosi' had returned a short piece in the *Evening Standard* dated 1st January 2000 in which it was reported that James Nkosi, aged forty-three, had died following a fall from a twelfth storey balcony. There had been no suspicious circumstances.

He thought of the child Ava had been, and of the incomprehensible loss that few people could truly understand—though he happened to be one of the few.

At the last moment, he jabbed the button for Ava's floor.

Ava looked at her own face in the bathroom mirror.

She saw a pallid complexion and eyes that were over-bright with fear, but also anticipation. Her face was younger than it was now, unblemished by tiny lines that fanned out on either side of her eyes, and her hair was a mass of dark brown curls, unfaded by the passage of time.

You can do this, she heard herself say.

The bathroom was small and impersonal, all white except for a mint-green towel hanging from a rail beside the sink. In the corner of the shower enclosure, she saw a bottle of *Head and Shoulders for Men,* and another bottle containing mint-infused body wash. She felt sick, and waves of nausea had her gripping the sink.

Once the feeling passed, she reached for the door handle and stepped out into a narrow corridor. There were no pictures on the walls, nor any personal mementos, but her feet guided her towards a living room where she found two men chatting over a glass of red wine.

"There she is," Ian O' Shea said.

He turned, and she saw the front of his shirt was soaked in blood, which ran from a gaping wound at his neck. His eyes, which had once been a beautiful shade of blue, were now filmed white.

"She's a looker, isn't she?" DI Lipman said, as white foam dribbled from the corner of his mouth and down onto his naked chest.

"I was falling in love with her," Ian said, conversationally.

"Bad luck, mate," Lipman said, and clinked glasses.

A primal scream rose up in her chest, but no sound came out of her mouth.

"Ava?"

She awoke with a start, her body trembling all over.

"It's okay," Alex said, and held her shoulders in a gentle grip. "You're at the hospital, you're safe here."

"I—they were *dead*."

"Who was dead?" he asked, softly.

"The men in my dream," she said, and dragged herself into a seated position, wiping sweat from her brow. "One of them was Ian O' Shea, I think."

"What did he look like?"

"Blond, good-looking, with—with blue eyes," she said, but they'd been white in the dream. "He had blood all down his shirt, and his neck—"

She swallowed, and reached out a shaking hand for the glass of water at her bedside.

Alex helped her, and, once she'd drained the glass, refilled it for her.

"I don't know who the other man was," she said. "But I can describe him—"

"Just a minute," Alex said, and grabbed the notebook she kept beside her bed. "I'll write down whatever you tell me, so we don't forget it later."

"Thanks," she said, and closed her eyes to recall his image. "He was older than Ian, maybe his fifties? He didn't look well...he was overweight, and his face was covered in thread veins. I thought he might be an alcoholic, or something like that."

Alex nodded, and made swift notes. "Was he taller than Ian?"

"Um...no, he was a few inches shorter," she said, focusing on the dimming memory of what she'd seen.

"Think about his face again," Alex said. "What was his skin tone—Caucasian?"

She nodded. "Yes, he was white," she said. "He had thinning, grey hair."

"What about clothing? What was he wearing?"

"Um, dark trousers," she said.

"What about on top?"

"Nothing," she said. "He was bare-chested."

Interesting, Alex thought, and made a note. "You said he was dead," he said. "How do you know? Was he bleeding, like Ian?"

She shook her head.

"He had foam coming out of his mouth," she said. "I don't know how I knew he was dead … I just did."

"Okay," Alex said, and decided to move onto less traumatic imagery. "What about the setting? Where were they?"

"In an apartment," she said, without hesitation. "A new build, with pale laminate wood flooring and white walls. Sitting on a black leather sofa. It smelled of cigarettes."

"You're doing very well," Alex said. "Try to keep going. Do you remember anything else about it?"

"I—I remember a bathroom," she said. "It was white, just like the walls. I was looking in the mirror and feeling sick."

"You saw yourself in the mirror?"

"Yes," she whispered.

"How old were you?"

She raised a hand to rub her aching head. "I—I don't know," she muttered. "Younger than I am, now. Twenty-something?"

Alex closed the notebook and set it back on the bedside table.

"It sounds as though your mind has muddled two crime scenes together. I don't know whether Carter has already told you this, but you were the one to find Ian's body at his flat, so it's no surprise that you have a clear memory of how he might have looked. As for the other man, it sounds as though he belongs to another time—perhaps another case you worked on, when you were first starting out in Major Crimes?"

She nodded thoughtfully. "Yes, that would make sense," she said. "What about the apartment, and the bathroom?"

"I could ask Carter to show you some of the interior shots of Ian's flat, so you can compare it with your dream," Alex offered. "It may have been his place you were imagining."

For some reason, she doubted it, but it didn't hurt to rule it out. "Yes, that might help."

"We could also ask him to look over some old case files from your early days to see if there's a victim that matches the description of the older man?"

"I don't know why I'm remembering all of these awful things," she said.

"Because you're a murder detective," he said. "Your work is a huge part of your life, and you saw images like the ones in your dream every day. It may feel awful now, because it seems like the first time you're seeing death, but you've dealt with it in some form or another for years."

He paused, allowing that to sink in, and then raised a more sensitive topic.

"Have you had any further memories about your brother, or your father?"

She shook her head. "I spoke with my mother, and she told me a bit more about—about the circumstances."

He said nothing, and she smiled.

"I take it, you already know?"

"I found something on the Internet," he admitted. "It listed your family name as 'Nkosi', rather than 'Hope'."

At his mention of the name, she had another flash memory.

This time, of a man dressed in a t-shirt and jogging pants, sitting on the floor of an old kitchen.

Nkosi, he said. *You're Ava Nkosi.*

She blinked, and found Alex watching her again. "Another memory?"

She nodded. "Yes—I—I think I used to be called Ava Nkosi," she said. "My mother remarried after my father died, and her new husband is Benjamin Hope. Maybe I changed my name when she did, to have a fresh start."

"Maybe," he agreed.

She looked across at him with frightened eyes. "It feels as though the memories are getting... *closer*," she said. "I can sense it, Alex. They're coming back a lot more regularly, especially in my sleep. I'm frightened of remembering that day, when Carl shot me—and Naomi."

He reached across and took her hand in a supportive grip. "It might feel frightening but, just remember, you survived," he said. "You're here, living and breathing, whereas Carl Deere is dead and buried. He can't hurt you, ever again. All you'd be remembering is an echo of the past."

She nodded, and looked down at their hands to find hers covered in blood again.

She let go of his fingers and tucked hers beneath the bedclothes.

Just a hallucination, she told herself. *That's all it is.*

"I'll see you tomorrow," he said. "You can call me, any time."

Ava nodded, and watched her friend leave to go in search of the woman he loved.

Tut, tut, the voice whispered again.

You've been a naughty girl.

CHAPTER 29

Ben Carter made his way past the British Museum, battling through the late afternoon crowd of tourists towards Russell Square. The sun was already making its descent, and the skies above London were a melting pot of golden hues, but he didn't stop to look up. He walked briskly through the streets and entered the square, making his way directly towards one of the wooden benches in the north-east corner, where a woman dressed in a long winter coat was already seated reading a magazine.

He sat beside her.

"I suppose, you couldn't have chosen somewhere *indoors*," she remarked. "It's bloody cold out here, Carter."

"Sorry, ma'am. It's all I could think of."

She turned the page of her magazine with one gloved finger. "Well?" she demanded. "Why the sudden urgency?"

"I spoke with Doctor Gregory this morning," he said, watching the dog-walkers and pedestrians who passed by. "He thinks Ava's memory could return in full, because he doesn't believe she's suffering from anterograde amnesia. He thinks it's all to do with trauma and, if she can get past that, the memories will come back."

"I'm happy for her," his contact said. "How does that help us?"

"It doesn't," Carter said. "But there's a safeguarding issue, because she's in the same hospital as Naomi Palmer. If Ava was the one who attacked her, then she may want to finish the job."

"In a hospital?" his contact scoffed. "Ava wouldn't have the nerve for it. She could be seen by any number of people."

"She's been hiding in plain sight for years," Carter argued. "As for Palmer, she's so vulnerable, it would only take the flick of a switch. I think Ava should be transferred elsewhere, as a precaution, since Naomi can't be safely moved."

"And what, exactly, would we tell her? *Sorry, love, but we think you're a murderer, so we want to move you just in case you can't help yourself?* That would scupper three years of careful work."

Carter blew into his hands, to warm them. "We can think of a cover story," he said. "Bed management at the hospital, or something like that."

"It doesn't solve our main problem, which is that we have insufficient evidence of wrongdoing," his contact said. "We need to force her hand, or we've got nothing."

It pained him to admit it, but she was right. He'd been over the files more times than he could count, but there'd been no 'Eureka!' moment that would provide the evidence they needed; only a series of coincidences that any defence team would rip to shreds.

"How do you suggest we do that?" he asked.

"It's your job to figure that out," she said, and came to her feet. "Use whatever means at your disposal."

On which note, she left him to think it over.

Carter's 'Eureka!' moment came unexpectedly in the form of a telephone call from Doctor Gregory.

"Ben? It's Alex. I wonder if I could have your help with something?"

"You been done for indecent exposure again, Doc? Because I can't keep bailing you out, like this."

Alex grinned. "Not this time," he said. "Actually, it's really to help Ava."

Carter's ears sharpened. "Oh? What can I do?"

"She seems to be remembering past cases, but the details are all jumbled," Alex said. "It would help her to be able to organise the memories, in her own mind. I was thinking, if you were able to match up some of the descriptions she's given to real cases, that might be a stepping stone."

Carter told himself not to get too excited. "What—ah—what kind of descriptions did she give?" he asked.

"Well, for instance, she had a dream about two men, one of whom she recognised as being Ian O'Shea, but the other one she couldn't recollect at all."

"If she can remember some of the physical details, I'm sure I can try to match them up."

"I made a note of some of it," Gregory said, and Carter sent up a silent prayer of thanks. "She's pretty exhausted, so I don't think we should bother her with anything more today, but I could come by The Yard?"

"I've already finished my shift for today," Carter said. "I'll drop by your place in around an hour, if that works for you."

He ended the call and wondered whether, after three long years, his luck had finally changed.

An hour later, Carter arrived on Gregory's doorstep with some old cardboard files tucked underneath his arm.

"Come in," Alex said. "Something to drink? To eat?"

It was rare that Carter couldn't force down a snack of some description, but he was too wired to think of food.

"I wouldn't say no to a coffee," he said, and tapped the files. "I thought we could take a look at some possibilities."

"Good idea," Alex said, and led him towards the living room, where Bill Douglas was reclining on the sofa reading a copy of *The Week*.

"Ben!" he said. "Good to see you."

"Professor. I heard you found the missing kid?"

Alex set about making a pot of coffee in the adjoining kitchen.

"Yes, thank goodness," Douglas replied. "It seems the boy's elder brother was responsible, with some help from a girlfriend."

Carter made a huffing sound in his chest, which might have signified any number of emotions. "It's always somebody close, or within the family," he said. "What was the motive?"

"Money," Alex called out. "But the true motive was jealousy, mingled with a generous dose of narcissism, I'll venture to say."

"Seconded," Douglas put in. "I'd be interested to read the psychological evaluation of both boys, but that's for another day. I hear that Ava has remembered some details from her past?"

"Past cases," Alex corrected him, and set down three mugs of coffee. "We're hoping to flesh out the memories with some names and dates, to help her. If she can put her memories into chronological order, somehow, then it might spark new ones."

He reached for some notes he'd taken after leaving Ava at the hospital, which were an exact copy of the notes he'd scribbled in her journal.

"Here," he said, handing them to Carter. "Take a look, and see if anything jumps out at you."

Ben took the papers and sat down, saying nothing as his eyes raced over the words on the page.

"You're sure this is what she said?"

Alex nodded. "I'd forgotten to tear out the page from her journal to give to you, but I didn't want to disturb Ava again, so I stopped by the hospital shop and picked up a pad of paper to write it all down while everything was still fresh in my mind,' he said. "I don't think I've mistaken or embellished anything, but you can easily check it against the original note, next time you're visiting."

Carter nodded, and looked back at the page.

"As I said on the phone, the younger of the two men in her dream seems to match the description of Ian O' Shea, and Ava thought that, herself," Alex said. "Do you have any idea who the other man could be?"

Oh, yes, Carter thought.

"Possibly," he replied. "Without a cause of death, it's difficult to say, but she's given a good physical description of the man, so that's helpful."

"Ava seemed to think she was younger at the time of the man's death," Alex pointed out. "She said 'twenty-something', which means anything between ten and, maybe, eighteen years ago?"

Bill leaned forward and held out a hand.

"Mind if I take a look?"

Since they were both *technically* still on the Met's payroll, Carter handed over the paperwork.

"Interesting that the older man wasn't wearing anything on top," Bill remarked.

The missing piece of a jigsaw clicked softly into place, in Carter's mind. "*What did you say?*"

"The man in her dream," Bill repeated. "It's odd that he wasn't wearing anything on his top half, but she says he had dark trousers on, so he wasn't completely naked."

Carter knew that DI Lipman's body had been found bare-chested and collapsed on the sofa in his flat, with his own belt wrapped tightly around his upper arm and a syringe hanging from one of the veins. Police Constable Ava Hope, as she'd been then, had given a statement to say that Lipman had dropped her at the tube station at the end of their evening shift and that was the last time she'd seen him alive; certainly, she'd never worked at his crime scene, and Carter had already run a security check to see whether she'd accessed Lipman's file on their internal computer system—which she hadn't, because Ava was smart and careful.

Therefore, there was no way she could have known about Lipman's state of undress unless she'd seen it with her own eyes. *But somebody who'd worked the case might have told her,* the defence would argue.

He needed more.

"She remembered some detail about the apartment," he said, going back over the notes. "But it could describe any number of new-builds in the city, including Ian O'Shea's."

It didn't help him, since it was already common knowledge that Ava had visited O'Shea's apartment, and therefore had good reason to remember it in her dream. However, if she remembered DI Lipman's old apartment, that would be something else entirely…

"I wonder if you could ask her for more detail about the décor, the walls, the colour of the sofa—" he began.

"Oh, I'm sorry, I must have forgotten to write that down," Alex muttered, a bit annoyed with himself. "She said it was black leather."

Carter smiled beautifully. "In that case, she wasn't describing Ian O'Shea's apartment," he said, and reached for the files he'd brought. "Just a minute."

He opened one entitled, 'LIPMAN' and flicked through the pages until he came to a series of photographs taken from the crime scene at the dead man's flat, back in 2012. The image quality was poor, since they were copied from the originals, but still, they did the job.

Carter laid them out on the coffee table in front of the other two men, and they angled their heads to look at grainy pictures of a bare-chested man in his fifties, slumped against a black sofa with vomit and other fluids crusted against his torso. A brown leather belt hung from his upper arm, and a spent syringe lay flaccidly against his skin.

"That looks like a pretty good match to Ava's description," Alex said, but then his brow furrowed. "How did you know to bring this file, in particular, Ben? There must have been thousands of cases Ava's worked on, over the years."

Carter performed a swift cost-benefit analysis, and came to a decision.

All means at your disposal, his boss had said.

"DI Lipman was a longstanding member of the Major Crimes division, who died following an apparent overdose on a bad batch of heroin, back in 2012," he said.

"I see," Bill replied. "Was Ava part of the investigating team?"

Carter gave him the ghost of a smile. "No, she was a new member of his section," he replied. "Ava was working a shift with him, the night he died."

Alex held up his hands. "Sorry," he said. "I don't think I'm following you. Was Ava there when he took the overdose?"

"No, according to her statement at the time, she was miles away, tucked up at home," Carter replied.

"She must have remembered his image from seeing the file, I suppose," Alex said. "Transferred memories can be deceptive."

"Ava has never accessed the file, and never worked on the case in any capacity," Carter said, and waited for the penny to drop.

"Then, how—" Alex started to say.

"How could she describe Lipman's flat, and his body?" Carter finished for him. "That's a question I've been trying to answer since I transferred onto her team, over three years ago."

There was a short, humming silence.

"You're saying, you believe Ava was somehow involved in this—Lipman's—death?" Bill said, with an air of disbelief. "That can't be possible. She's one of the most honourable people we've ever met."

Carter took his time formulating a reply, because Douglas wasn't wholly wrong in his assessment of the woman they'd come to know. "Ava Hope is a person of two halves," he said. "As a Met detective, she's one of the best. She's closed more cases and brought justice to many more families than several other officers combined. But there's another side to her, one that predates the *honourable* detective."

"Go on," Alex said, in a tone that was oddly devoid of emotion.

"You already know Ava had a brother, and that he was murdered," Carter said, and both men nodded. "You may have seen some articles written at the time, which paint the picture of a young dealer who ran with the wrong crowd and got what was coming to him."

He gave a small shake of his head.

"The truth is, Daniel had *no* links with any of the gangs in his area, and no history of either selling or using drugs," he continued.

"The family always maintained that, but the police found a bag of hash on his body and came to their own conclusions. Maybe it was planted on him by the investigating officers."

"Why would they do that?" Bill asked, horrified.

"To protect the gang who killed him," Carter said. "If they were in business, the last thing any bent copper would have wanted is for that income stream to dry up, which it might have done, if their contacts were behind bars for murder."

He paused to take a drink of his coffee.

"If we assume there was an interest to protect, that explains why the investigation was deliberately shoddy," he said. "Witnesses were overlooked, processes and leads weren't followed. Vital evidence was probably lost, simply because it wasn't collected when it should have been. Names of likely perpetrators were given but not chased up, or even interviewed. In short, it was a very bad job, and the family had every right to feel let down by the system—added to which, there was a strong racial flavour to the whole thing, which tallies with a broader, institutional attitude that was prevalent in The Yard at the time."

"Where does Lipman come into all this?" Bill asked.

"He was part of the original investigating team," Alex guessed, and Carter nodded.

"Yes. He and another detective, Sergeant Vaughn, who is—"

"Also dead," Alex surmised, and put a hand to his head while his mind caught up with what his heart already suspected. "Isn't he?"

"Four years after Lipman," Carter confirmed. "In an apparent gang shooting, at his home. Lipman and Vaughn were part of a widespread internal investigation that was mounted after the new Police Commissioner came into post, in 2020. The idea was to clean up corruption at The Yard."

"I take it, that's where you come in?" Bill said.

Carter smiled. "Lipman and Vaughn's names came up again and again," he said. "I knew they were already dead, but their legacy might not be, so I had to be thorough. It was only as I was looking into their past handiwork that

I started to wonder about the circumstances of their deaths. Ava's name came up, as a member of their team, so I checked her out—again, just to be thorough. That's when I found out she'd changed her name from Nkosi, and of course I tugged that line and found out what happened to her brother. What interested me, most of all, was the fact that Lipman and Vaughn had led the original investigation into his murder."

He went on to talk about two of the gang members who'd also died, in apparent overdoses.

"You think she killed all of them?" Alex asked him.

"Yes, I do."

"Why haven't you arrested her, then?" Bill said, looking aggrieved.

"Lack of evidence," Carter said, with a shrug. "All I had was a series of bad coincidences, until just now."

"Her description of Lipman and his apartment," Alex realised, and rested his forearms on his knees. "She shouldn't have known anything about it."

"She claimed never to have been to his place," Carter said. "She says so in her statement, right here, in black and white." He pointed at the file on the table.

"What now?" Bill asked. "She still doesn't remember any of it."

"Are you sure?"

"Are you?" Alex countered. "Are you sure about *any* of this, Ben? It's a hell of an accusation to make about your colleague, and it'll be a long way to fall, if you're wrong."

Carter looked him dead in the eye. "I'm not wrong," he said. "And I think I know how to prove it."

CHAPTER 30

Irene Hope cast a worried eye over her daughter. "You're not sleeping," she said.

Ava didn't like to say that the other three patients on her ward all snored like steam trains, in case they should overhear and be offended. "It's just the hospital environment," she said. "Hopefully, I'll be out of here soon."

"Has the consultant told you when that'll be?" Irene asked.

"No, but my memories are coming back now," she said. "Mostly, old cases."

"That's good news," her mother said, but Ava thought of the dead men she'd dreamed about, and shuddered. "Mum—"

"Well, I must be going," her mother said. "Your father will be needing his dinner."

"He's not my father."

"You know what I mean," Irene said.

Ava closed her eyes, and an image of James Nkosi swam in front of her eyes. Tall, handsome and dark-skinned, she could feel the warmth of his body beside hers as they worked through a maths puzzle together.

Well done, Princess! You're a smart cookie.

Her eyes opened again, misted with tears. "Dad was good at maths, wasn't he?"

Irene stuck her arms in her woollen overcoat, and gave a jerky nod. "Yes," she replied, huskily. "He was good at many things."

Irene sank back down on the visitor's chair.

"He had a beautiful voice," she said.

"He loved Pavarotti," Ava remembered. "He used to sing *Nessun Dorma* around the flat."

Irene nodded and then, dashing the moisture from her eyes, stood up again. "I have to go, now."

"Okay. Thank you for coming."

Irene paused, and turned back to put a hand on her daughter's cheek. "I—I'm sorry, Ava."

"For what?"

"I wasn't there," she said. "When Daniel died, he took a piece of my soul with him. I was there in body but not in spirit, and I forgot how to be a mother to you. I'm sorry about that."

Ava's throat worked as she fought back tears. "It's all right," she managed.

"I used to look at you, sometimes, and wonder where my little girl went," Irene whispered. "For such a long time, you seemed so *hard*. These past few weeks, it's as though you've come back to me. Everything is new again and you're rediscovering the world. I hope you stay that way, for a while longer."

Ava swallowed the emotion that threatened to choke her. "Nothing stays the same forever," she said.

Ava watched the woman throw herself against a wall, again and again, as hard as she could.

She felt the painful throb of it each time her head cracked against brick and plaster; the burn of skin tearing open and the trickle of blood running down her cheek. She saw a Latin acrostic written on a wall, with some of the letters circled in green and some of the words rubbed out. She saw Doctor Gregory's timeline and the notes he'd made, and pictures of men and women who were already dead—all apart from a man whose face stared back at her with a knowing expression in his cold eyes. She knew he would be dead within a matter of days... but, not yet. He was still at large, and could be anywhere.

She looked down at the floor where Naomi Palmer lay motionless, her head weeping blood onto the carpet. A police-issued Glock rested nearby, the butt of the weapon coated in red.

Her weapon, Ava thought. *Naomi's blood.*

The woman stopped hitting herself against the wall and turned around, startled by a noise.

She looked straight through Ava, and, in her dream, Ava turned to find a man standing behind her, the same man she recognised from the picture on the wall.

Carl Deere.

He held the gun in his hand and said something to the woman. Ava swung back to look at her, but found only an empty wall covered in bloodstains.

The woman had gone.

There was nobody else in the room aside from Naomi, whose inert body still lay on the pale carpet at the foot of the bed.

"I'm sorry," Ava whispered to her.

Carl lifted the gun and trained it at her head.

Tut, tut, he said, and tipped it back and forth.

"I can explain," she told him, although no sound came from her lips. "We can come to an arrangement."

He shook his head, and she threw up a hand as if she could stop the bullet that was about to fly through the air and puncture her brain. Nothing could stop that, she knew, because this was all in the past; a memory of what had already happened and could not be changed.

Carl pulled the trigger, and she braced herself for impact.

For the second time that day, Ava awoke with a scream, and found Gregory waiting beside the bed.

"Take it easy," he said, helping her into a seated position. "Do you want some water?"

She shook her head. "No—no, thanks. What time is it?"

"Seven-thirty," he replied, after a quick check. "I thought I'd stop in and see how you're doing, after this morning."

She rubbed a hand over her face. "I had another vivid dream," she said. "It was very similar to the one I had about the attack, yesterday."

"But not identical?"

She shook her head. "No. This time, I saw Carl Deere's face, and I—" she started to tell him about the woman she'd seen, the one who'd been hitting her head against the walls.

Then, the truth came crashing down.

She was that woman.

She raised a shaking hand to her head, trying to make sense of it.

"What did you see?" Alex prompted her.

"I—I saw Carl," she said. "And Naomi, lying on the floor."

Next to your gun, her mind whispered. *What did you do, Ava?*

What did you do?

"Did you see Carl attack Naomi?"

Ava shook her head. "I didn't see what happened to Naomi."

Yes, you did.

You know exactly what happened to Naomi.

She closed her eyes, fighting the memories that were knocking upon her door, demanding to be let in.

*I don't think Carl Deere murdered Ian O' Shea...*Naomi had said.

"Ava?"

She looked across at Alex, who was watching her with a worried expression marring his handsome face.

"Is everything okay? You look as if you'd seen a ghost."

"I'm just tired," she said. "I think that's enough for today."

He was about to say something else, when the door to the ward opened and one of the nurses from Naomi's floor stepped inside, looking as if she'd run all the way up the stairs.

"Doctor Gregory? Oh, thank goodness, I thought you might've gone home," she said, breathlessly.

"Not yet," he said. "Is everything all right?"

"It's Naomi," she said. "She woke up, and was asking for you."

Gregory was on his feet in seconds. "*What*? I'll come now—"

But the nurse held up a hand. "We had to sedate her," she told him. "She kept saying she had something very important she needed to tell you. She was becoming very upset about it, and her heart rate was rising dangerously, so the doctor took the decision to calm her system down. She's sleeping now, but I thought you'd want to know, since it's such a big development."

Gregory looked across at Ava, who was listening intently. "I can hardly believe it," he said, happily. "I wonder what she wanted to tell me…but, that doesn't matter. What matters most is that she's come around, and that she asked for me. It means the damage isn't as bad as we feared."

Ava smiled. "Yes, that's wonderful news."

"Naomi will probably sleep until morning," the nurse said. "If you come back first thing, there's every chance she'll be awake again—you can speak to her, then."

Alex dragged in a shaky breath, overcome by emotion. "Yes, all right," he said. "Can I come and say 'goodnight' to her?"

The nurse checked the time, and then nodded. "If you're quick," she said. "Visiting hours are almost over."

Alex turned back to Ava. "I'll come and see you again tomorrow," he said, gathering up his coat. "Don't try to fight the memories; just let them come. It'll be less traumatic, that way."

Ava looked down at her hands, and imagined they were covered in blood. "Alex?"

"Yes?"

"Have you ever had a patient who was beyond your help?"

He thought instantly of his mother, and gave a smile that didn't quite reach his eyes. "I don't believe *anybody* is beyond help," he said. "Why do you ask?"

Ava swallowed, and looked away. "You should say 'goodbye' to Naomi," she said. "It's getting late."

CHAPTER 31

All was quiet at the hospital, aside from the incessant snores that ricocheted around the walls of Ava's ward. For once, she welcomed the sound, which kept her awake and alert until the early hours of the morning. By then, most of the in-patients were asleep, while the clinical staff tended to emergencies or retreated to the break room to make successive rounds of sugary tea. She'd spent hours debating with herself, knowing what she had to do, but no longer sure that she could do it.

You've done it before, she told herself.

Yes, but everything is different, now. You're different.

Whilst the ignorance of the past few weeks had been blissful, Ava couldn't lay claim to it any longer. What had begun as a trickle of lost memories had become a tidal wave, from which there was no escape. Her mind had protected itself for as long as it could, hiding behind the trauma of her injuries, but the veil had lifted and taken with it any possible doubt—or hope—she might've had about her own nature.

She remembered everything.

Ava could recall every detail of her brother's face, his voice and his laugh. She loved him and grieved for him all over again; the pain of his passing as raw as had been on that miserable night in 1995. She felt her parents' suffering and remembered the anger that had built, week by week, month by month, and year upon year, until it was a burning hellfire in the cavity where her heart should have been. Her rage had been renewed, and demanded satisfaction.

Ava knew that she'd killed five people, almost six. She also knew that the journey she'd begun all those years ago was not yet complete, and she would need to kill again, to balance the scales. She felt no sadness; only an initial shock that was soon overtaken by the righteous knowledge that she'd be able to bring about some kind of justice for Daniel, where the system had failed. It was the only reason she'd joined the Metropolitan Police—to put herself within reach of the men who'd failed her family, and have them pay for it.

Why did you stay in the Force, after Lipman and Vaughn were gone? You could have left, if you hate the system, so much.

She ignored the voice inside her mind, and quietly slipped out of bed. It was unhygienic to wander around the hospital corridors barefoot, but her slippers would be loud by comparison and so, with a delicate wrinkle of her nose, Ava tiptoed from the room.

Outside, the corridor was empty. Somewhere in the distance, she heard a YouTube video being played or, perhaps, some detestable TikTok reel about cleaning or make-up contouring. Ignoring it, and the need for any walking aid, she made her way towards the stairwell, swift and sure-footed.

"Penny?"

Ava flattened herself against the wall as one of the senior nurses stepped halfway out of the break room, up ahead.

"Yes, chick?"

"Get us a sandwich, while you're down there, will yer? I'm clammin'."

The disembodied voice of one of the younger nurses filtered down the corridor, and Ava stood completely still.

"I'll get a selection," Penny said. "You fancy a brownie, as well?"

"Go on, then, you've twisted my arm."

Ava watched from the shadows, smiling slightly as Penny adjusted her bra strap before stepping into the lift and making her way down to the canteen, which was open twenty-four hours.

As the doors closed, she entered the stairwell.

Ava's hand gripped the banister as she hurried downstairs.

Given more time, she might have armed herself with a syringe. It would have been the easiest thing in the world to lift one from the medicine trolley as the dispensing nurse made her rounds, and then syphon off some of her own medication from the line they'd given her.

It might have taken a few days to collect a toxic dose, but she could have done it. Unfortunately, there was no time for any of that, so she'd have to make do with whatever means she could find.

See? her mind whispered. *You're no different, after all.*

You're the same as Paul Flint...

Her footsteps faltered, and she almost fell down the remaining stairs.

"I'm nothing like him. I don't get my kicks from murdering children. I don't *want* to hurt Naomi," she told the empty walls. "I *have* to do it."

No, you don't.

You don't have to kill her.

"I can't let her talk," Ava muttered.

Especially not before Flint was made to pay for his crimes. He was the last remaining member of the gang who'd killed her brother, and she'd waited such a long time. For a while, she'd even explored the possibility of gaining access to the prison where he'd been incarcerated, but that was far too risky, so she'd told herself to remain patient and wait for the day he was released.

What about your friend, Alex? He'll be heartbroken.

He'll recover, she told herself. He was resilient. In any event, she could console him, after the loss.

As you consoled Ian O' Shea? her mind taunted her. *He did nothing wrong, but you killed him anyway—*

"Shut up," she whispered, putting her hands to her ears. "Just, shut up. I don't want to think about it."

Ava came to Naomi's floor, cracked open the stairwell door and listened. She heard a trolley being wheeled along the corridor outside, followed by a friendly exchange between two of the staff, and waited until the squeaking wheels passed by before pushing the door open a little more.

She checked either end of the corridor, and then took her chance.

Ava made her way towards Naomi's room, sweating with the exertion.

Her legs were tired, but the power of 'mind over matter' was amazing, really. She told her body to move, and it did.

She told her body to kill, and it would.

If only she'd acted the previous day, before Naomi had woken up, she could have convinced herself it was an act of mercy. Killing a woman who was in a persistent vegetative state would have been a kindness. For goodness' sake, even beloved pets were given more dignity.

But Naomi *had* woken up, and it changed everything.

What's your excuse now?

Ava shoved the thought aside, and checked back over her shoulder as she approached Naomi's room. She looked through the window and saw a dark-haired woman lying on her side with her back to the door, probably having been turned by the nurses to avoid bedsores developing.

She covered the door handle with the edge of her pyjama top, and opened it.

The first thing she noticed was that some of the intravenous lines were no longer attached to

Naomi, now that she'd come out of her coma and was breathing independently. However, a SATs machine still monitored her oxygen intake, and a single line ran from the machine to her nose, where she was being fed oxygen through the night as a precaution.

She was still very weak.

Ava watched her sleeping form for a few minutes, her feet frozen to the floor.

Do it, she told herself. *Do it now, and leave!*

She took a step forward, then stopped again.

What are you waiting for? Get on with it!

Ava wiped sweat from her eyes, and took another step forward, then another, her silhouette illuminated only by the moon which shone brightly through the open curtains. She rounded the bed and turned the oxygen machine off completely, so that it wouldn't sound an alarm when the SATS dropped to a dangerous level. Then, very gently, she took Naomi's shoulder and rolled her onto her front, so that she was facedown against her own pillow.

Then, Ava gathered her nerve and leaned her body weight down, crushing Naomi's head into the pillow, waiting for the inevitable, automatic spasm that would follow—

The door to the shower room opened behind her, spreading a garish yellow light across the bed, casting her startled face into something clown-like.

"Step away," Carter said, coming fully into the room. "Move right back."

Meanwhile, the woman she'd thought was Naomi reared back from the pillow, thrusting her away.

Ava stumbled back, blinking as the main lights came on and Gregory entered the room, his eyes implacable, like chips of green ice.

She looked back at the woman on the bed, a young female police officer she didn't recognise but whose body shape and hair colour was a close match to Naomi Palmer's.

No, the voice whispered. *This can't be happening.*

You were so close.

So close—

Ava's pupils dilated, her heart rate thundered, and she collapsed.

Gregory rushed towards Ava, who hit the floor like a dead weight.

"She's unconscious," he pronounced. "Call a nurse."

He and Carter oversaw Ava's transfer onto the bed, and kept watch as she lay there trembling, her fingers clutching the edge of the pillow she'd recently tried to use as a means for murder. The young woman who'd acted as a stand-in for Naomi watched from across the room, and Carter jerked his chin in the direction of the corridor outside.

"You did well," he said. "You can head home, now. I'll get a statement from you, tomorrow."

"Cheers, Sarge," she said, and was gone.

He looked back at the woman on the bed, who continued to shake uncontrollably and mumbled words they couldn't understand.

"Ava?" Gregory said, and received no response. "Ava? Can you hear me?"

Carter watched him try a few more times, while gentle hands held her securely on the bed. "What's the matter with her?"

Alex straightened up, and shook his head. "I think she's had a psychotic break," he said. "You can arrest her, Ben, but she doesn't have capacity to acknowledge the standard caution, at the moment."

Carter swore, roundly. "I don't believe it," he said. "She just tried to kill someone—"

"Yes," Alex said. "We all witnessed it, so there's no question there. That doesn't change what's happened in her own mind."

A muscle ticked in Carter's jaw. "She isn't insane," he argued. "She could be faking it."

I don't think she is," Alex said, looking back at the woman he no longer recognised. "But she does need psychiatric care, and her defence will certainly argue diminished responsibility. You know they will."

Carter turned away, and paced around the room.

Three years, he thought.

Three long years.

"Does it really make a difference whether she's incarcerated in Southmoor Hospital or a maximum-security prison?" Alex wondered. "Either way, she won't be a danger to society."

Carter blew out a long breath. "You're right," he said. "That has to be worth something. At least our plan worked."

Gregory looked down at Ava, then away. "I don't think there are any winners, here," he said, and thought of Naomi, who had not woken up—she never had. She remained in a coma, sleeping peacefully in a different bed further down the hall. They'd moved her earlier that evening, having first enlisted the help of a nurse to impart false news of her recovery so that Ava would believe it, and be forced to act.

"I'm sorry," Carter said. "I wasn't thinking."

"I wanted the subterfuge to be real," Alex said, softly. "I wanted to believe Naomi had woken up."

Carter crossed the room to put a hand on his shoulder. "One day, she might…"

"Yeah," Alex said. "One day."

He looked at the woman who was responsible for it all, and tried to find the clinical detachment he needed to prevent himself from wringing her miserable neck.

He was only human, after all.

CHAPTER 32

One week later

A light drizzle fell over the Houses of Parliament as Gregory and Douglas made their way to the offices of Jonathan Smythe MP, for a second time. They managed to arrive ahead of the man himself, but not before Chief Constable Porter, who was already seated in the waiting room.

"Well, if it isn't Starsky and Hutch," he drawled.

It wasn't intended as a compliment, but Douglas took it as one, anyway. "Which one of us do you see as Starsky, and which as Hutch?"

Porter favoured him with a fulminating glare.

"Uh-oh," Douglas said, in a stage whisper.

"When we last met in these offices, it was my understanding that we would work collaboratively," Porter said, in clipped tones.

"That was also our understanding," Gregory replied, taking one of the empty chairs.

"Indeed? In that case, perhaps you'd care to explain your reasoning for taking the unilateral decision to break into Daisy Richmond's home, without choosing to inform us, first?"

Ah, Gregory thought, and took a deep breath.

"In the first instance, DCI Verrill *was* informed of our suspicion that Rory Smythe was being held at Daisy's house," he replied. "I advised Mr Smythe to await the arrival of the police, but he was determined to go there and rescue his son, with or without our help. On balance, I felt there would be greater safety in numbers, since wild horses weren't going to stop him." He paused. "I certainly wouldn't have wanted to waste valuable police time following a profiling wild goose chase," he said, pointedly. "Besides, when we heard Rory crying out for help, there was no choice but to enter."

"You were extremely lucky the situation ended as well as it did," Porter muttered.

"You know, by resolving the situation as they did, Mr Smythe has managed to avoid any unsavoury public exposure," Douglas mused. "In fact, some might say, it could be extremely *beneficial* for a Chief Constable to have an MP sitting on the Home Affairs Select Committee who owes him a favour or two."

Porter opened his mouth, and then shut it again. "I—that's entirely beside the point."

"Furthermore," Douglas continued, in the same soothing voice, "by avoiding formal interviews of Rory ahead of any public prosecution, some might say that you've saved the boy from any additional trauma, which is another reason for his parents to be grateful. Arguably, it's a purely domestic matter, rather than a kidnapping case, in any event."

Porter scowled at them both, but was afforded a reprieve when the outer door opened and Smythe strode into the room with his aide a couple of steps behind him.

"Apologies for my tardiness," he said, and led them through to his office, where he opened a small drinks cabinet and took out five glasses, into which he sloshed a few fingers of aged whisky.

"I know you're on duty," he said. "So am I, if it comes to that, but there's reason to celebrate. I have my son back."

He didn't mention Theo, and neither did they.

"I'm sure, just this once—" Porter said, and raised his glass to tap it against Smythe's. "I speak for the whole force when I say we're very glad Rory is safely back at home, where he belongs."

"We all are," Bill added.

"I want to thank you all, individually, for the part you played in finding Rory," Smythe said.

"How's he doing?" Alex asked him.

Smythe looked at his glass, and set it down.

"He's okay," he replied. "The doctors say there's no lasting damage, although he was very tired and groggy this morning. Mainly, he was frightened and confused. It seems Daisy and Theo allowed him to play Nintendo and eat pizza for most of the time, under the guise of it being an elaborate prank, which, of course, he was happy to play along with. They drugged him when one or both of them had to leave the house or when they were afraid he might be overheard by Daisy's neighbour."

The thought of what might have happened was unbearable, and even more distressing than what *had* happened.

"Theo claims he never intended for things to escalate so quickly," he said. "Apparently, he's sorry." Smythe lifted a shoulder, which conveyed what he thought of that sentiment. "He wanted the money for a gap year, which I'd already refused," he explained. "I told him, I had no intention of funding a useless year spent in Thailand or wherever else, where he'd claim to work in an orphanage while partying on the beach and snorting God only knows what up his nose. I told him to get a job, if he wasn't planning to go straight to university, which didn't go down well at the time."

He folded his arms.

"Of course, the main reason was that he's still angry with me for abandoning him and his mother, or so he thinks."

"What do you intend to do?" Porter asked him.

Smythe picked up his drink again. "Anita and I can't bring ourselves to press charges against him," he said, and thought of Camilla, who'd begged him not to. "However, Theo deserves to be punished for what he did; not only for his own sake, but so that Rory knows I won't stand for that behaviour, and that I'll always protect him. It would be the same, if the situation were reversed."

He knocked back the whisky, and set the glass down again.

"We've found Theo a gap year placement in rural Nepal, where he'll spend twelve months working for a charity that builds sanitation infrastructures. It'll be back-breaking work, so they've assured me, and just the thing to build character."

Gregory said nothing, but there must have been a question in his eyes, because Smythe answered it.

"I acknowledge that I haven't been the father to Theo that I've been to Rory," he said. "I know that, on some level, this whole debacle was a cry for attention. That being the case, I've resolved to make changes to my own character, too. I'll be going out to Nepal to visit Theo every few weeks, and we'll build something together. He leaves next week—unless you need him to stay for any reason, Chief Constable?"

All eyes turned to Porter, who considered the public interest in prosecuting such a case, and then shook his head.

"Sometimes, good policing means taking a 'hands off' approach," he said. "As Rory was unharmed, and there doesn't appear to be any wider public safety issue, I'm content to leave this in the hands of your family to deal with, Mr Smythe, with the proviso that Theo is given the appropriate mental health support."

"Of course," his father said. "We've already enlisted the help of an eminent psychiatrist, on the recommendation of Doctor Gregory and Professor Douglas."

Porter might have known they'd be one step ahead. "That's gratifying to know," he said.

"Well, my thanks to you gentlemen, once again," Smythe said. "I'm afraid I'm late for my next engagement, so I must leave you now.

Chief Constable? I look forward to seeing you at the forthcoming budget meeting." He sent Porter a meaningful look.

"I look *forward* to it," he replied.

Smythe made for the door, before remembering something else. "Doctor Gregory, Professor Douglas, I want to say again how much your efforts were appreciated by my wife and me," he said. "The whole matter was handled with sensitivity and discretion throughout, and your insights about the perpetrator—about Theo—were proven to be largely correct, as they were in the case of Carl Deere. It occurs to me that a dedicated profiling unit would be highly beneficial, especially in complex and serious cases. Certainly, if the Chief Constable were to seek further funding for such a unit, it would be looked upon favourably by the Committee."

He looked to Porter for confirmation.

"I—yes, yes, I'm sure that would be—very useful," he finished, lamely.

"Splendid. I'll look forward to receiving your proposal," Smythe said.

As the door closed behind him, Porter turned to find Gregory and Douglas smiling like a pair of Cheshire cats.

"Oh, bugger off," he said, and made them all laugh.

Douglas gave him a friendly clap on the back. "How about a bite to eat?" he said. "I know a lovely little Greek place, not far from here, where we can share a mezze while we talk about staffing and resources for our new profiling unit."

Porter looked across at Gregory. "Is this how he reels people in?"

Alex thought of all the meals Bill had ever cooked for him, and had to wonder.

"They say the quickest way to a man's heart is through his stomach," Douglas said, and held the door open for them both. "I have a feeling we're all going to get along famously."

"I haven't agreed to any profiling unit, yet," Porter said, with a touch of desperation.

"See how you feel after some tzatziki," Bill replied, sagely.

The Chief Constable knew when he was beaten, and decided not to fight the tide any longer. "As it happens, there is a new case that may be of interest to you both," he said.

"We're all ears," Alex replied.

CHAPTER 33

Southmoor Hospital

Three months later

Southmoor Hospital was a desolate place, surrounded by high walls on all sides. It had been built during the Victorian era, when practicality and durability had been of paramount concern, rather than any finer aesthetic considerations. A number of wings led from a central block, like spokes on a bicycle wheel, and security rivalled that of the Houses of Parliament—which was understandable, considering the danger posed to the general public, should any of the hospital's residents manage to escape.

Alex thought this as he made his way through the security gates, stopping to share a friendly word with the guards whom he'd come to know during the ten years he'd spent working there. Everything about the place was familiar, from its smell—a combination of chemical bleach cleaning products and body odour—to its colourful walls, painted in turquoise and baby pink because somebody, sometime had claimed that it cheered an otherwise unruly and dangerous cohort of patients to see something besides white or beige.

"Alex!"

He paused in the act of collecting his belt and other personal effects from a security tray, and turned to find his old friend Parminder Aggarwal making her way down the corridor to greet him. As hospital director, she'd been a stalwart colleague during his tenure and, as a friend, she'd been an unfailing champion during good times and bad.

"Parminder," he said, warmly. "It's good to see you."

"And you, Alex, *and you*," she said, and gave him a hug. "It's been too long."

"It's been a challenging time," he admitted.

"Bill told me about Naomi," she said. "I'm so sorry."

He nodded.

"I confess, I was surprised that you'd come and visit Ava here," she said. "Are you sure you're ready?"

They began walking towards the wing where their latest resident was housed.

"I have some news for her," he said. "And I want to know what happened that day, with Naomi. I need to, for my sanity."

Parminder was an eternal optimist, which was a prerequisite for the position she held, but even her cheerful disposition knew the limitations of human nature. "You may not like what you hear," she warned him.

"I know," he admitted. "But still, I need to hear it."

"Bill also told me you've been granted funding to re-open a profiling unit," she said, after a moment. "I'm so pleased for you both, but I can't say we won't miss your skills here, on the ground."

He smiled. "It seems the mentally disordered tend to find me whether I'm in a hospital setting or not."

"We each have our cross to bear," she quipped. "Here we are."

They'd come to a secure meeting room, fully equipped to protect solicitors and other professionals from the vagaries of their clients.

"I can't offer you a hot drink, for obvious reasons, but how about some water? One of the nurses will bring Ava along in just a moment."

"No, thanks," he said. "I appreciate you arranging this, at short notice."

Parminder nodded, and, seeing the sadness that coated him like a shroud, gave in to the maternal instinct and hugged him one more time.

"Take care, Alex," she said. "While you're spending all your time helping others, don't forget to look after yourself, too."

The woman who entered the meeting room a few minutes later was not the Ava Hope he had come to know. Gone was the self-assured murder detective. In her place was a thin woman with shadowed eyes, which spoke of endless nights without sleep. She wore the ubiquitous garb of sweatpants and top, and her dark curly hair had been scraped back into a ponytail, leaving her face bare. There was a slight tremor to her hands, which he judged to be a common side-effect of the anti-psychotic medication she was likely to be taking, or else benzodiazepines for anxiety. She was accompanied by a security officer he recognised from the old days, and who gave him a brief smile before turning back to keep a sharp eye on his charge.

"Hello, Ava."

She stood beside the table, unsure whether to join him.

"Why don't you take a seat?" He gestured towards the chair opposite.

"Why—why are you here?" she whispered.

Alex had asked himself that question numerous times, but the answer remained nebulous. "To see you," he replied. "Sit down."

In the three months since she'd joined the community of staff and inmates at

Southmoor, Ava had become familiar with its strict routine, and, much like Pavlov's dogs, had also become responsive to a certain tone of command. Though he hadn't intended it, Alex adopted that tone, and she found herself obeying.

"How've you been?" he asked, once she'd settled herself.

She raised dark eyes to search his face. "You can't possibly care," she said.

He took the time to search his own heart, and formulate an honest reply.

"I care," he said. "I'm angry and disappointed by your actions, but I still care about whether your mind is recovering, Ava. You're unwell."

"No, I'm not."

But she looked at her hands, which were covered in blood again. She blinked several times, and the blood was gone.

"You have hallucinations," he said, and the quick look of shock told him he was correct. "Your doctors believe you may be suffering from schizophrenia, or another form of psychotic illness."

"That isn't why I killed those men," she said, very calmly.

Alex felt his chest tighten. "Why did you?" he asked her.

"You know why," she replied. "Revenge, justice, righting the scales. All of the above."

"And did you feel anything, when you did?"

"No," she replied. "Nothing except a feeling of…rightness."

"Did that also apply when you murdered Ian O' Shea?"

The small dart landed in her chest, and burrowed into her heart.

"That was…different."

"How?"

"He didn't deserve to die. I made a mistake."

"But the others weren't mistakes?"

"No."

It was fascinating, he thought, to hear her speak so candidly. Fascinating, and chilling, all at once.

"I thought he'd lied to me," she continued. "I thought Ian had played me for a fool, and that he was spying on me. That was Carter all along, wasn't it?"

He saw hatred in her eyes, and could only be glad for Ben Carter's sake that she was unlikely to be freed from the confines of the hospital for a long time to come. She'd made revenge an art form, and his betrayal was a capital offence.

"He has his duty to perform," Alex said. "You were a good detective, Ava. You must understand that, surely?"

Perhaps, Ava thought.

"My first duty is to my brother, and my family," she said. "My brother and father both died because of what those men did; whether it was the ones who kicked Daniel until his organs collapsed, or whether it was Lipman and Vaughn, who lied and covered up their crimes until my father was driven to suicide. They were all culpable and they'd have done it again and again, Alex, to other families. I know it, you know it, and Carter knows it, too. Don't speak to me about public duties; I've performed bigger acts of public service than either of you ever will."

"At what cost?" he asked, quietly. "You can't play God—none of us can."

She thought then of her mother, and of their last painful farewell before she'd left the hospital in a police van. "You wouldn't know—"

"Wouldn't I?" he said, and leaned forward so that she was forced to look at him. "I lost both of my siblings, Ava, and my entire family imploded. Every hour I spent in this hospital alongside the woman who'd killed them was a kind of torture, as was the knowledge that she wasn't a stranger, but my own mother. Do you think I couldn't have done as you did, and taken a syringe to her neck?"

She shook her head.

"Of course, I wanted to," he said, huskily. "I dreamed about it, sometimes, and lost a piece of my soul every time I even considered it. She was deeply unwell, as you are now, and the better part of me remembered that. If she'd had support, and help when she needed it, my mother would never have killed her own children. If you'd had the right support as a child, when you needed it in the aftermath of your brother's murder and your father's suicide, you wouldn't have walked along the destructive pathway that you did. You might have contented yourself with a meaningful profession helping others, and in doing so, you would have healed yourself."

A single tear escaped, and trailed down her face onto the table. "They killed him," she said.

"It isn't about what happens to us," he said, with devastating calm. "It's about how we respond to it. Why else do you think I'm here, speaking to you now, despite everything you've done?"

She sniffed, and he reached inside his pocket for a small packet of tissues.

"Thanks," she muttered, and blew her nose.

"I was sorry about Naomi," she said. "She and Ian weren't part of the plan."

His chest tightened, and a hard ball of anger settled in the pit of his stomach.

"I know," he managed to say.

"Is she—?"

"No," he said. "She hasn't woken up."

Ava decided to take the chance to purge herself, assuming that this would be the only visit he planned to make. "Naomi saw the inconsistency in your acrostic," she said.

"She knew that Ian O'Shea didn't fit, and she told me. She realised Carl Deere hadn't killed him."

"She didn't know she was confiding in the person who had."

Ava shook her head. "I—I know you won't believe me, but I'll say it anyway. I'm sorry."

Alex knew that, if she had the opportunity, she'd do it all again. He drew himself in, and focused on what he'd really come to say. "I came to tell you that Carter's lobbied, successfully, for an inquiry into the death of your brother."

Ava looked up, as more tears began to fall. "He—he did that? For me?"

Alex shook his head. "Not for you," he said. "He did it because it was the right thing to do. There are other ways to right the scales of justice, Ava—even if it takes longer than it should."

She held a hand across her eyes, and thought of Daniel. "My mother will be so happy," she said softly. "It's all she and my father ever wanted—due process, the same as everyone else."

He nodded, and cleared his throat.

"I have to go, now."

"Alex—"

He paused, waiting.

"Nothing," she whispered. "I hope—I hope Naomi recovers, that's all."

His eyes burned with unshed tears, and he gave a brief nod before turning away.

CHAPTER 34

Later that afternoon, Alex exchanged one hospital for another.

He would have known the route to Naomi's bedside blindfolded, and his legs worked on autopilot as he made his way through the entrance foyer to the bank of lifts, and then up to the floor where she'd already spent several weeks of her life wasting away into a white bedsheet while machines kept her body nourished and monitored her vital signs. When he arrived at her bedside, he found Bill Douglas there, reading to her from a book of poems by Seamus Heaney.

"Alex," he said, and closed the book. "I wasn't sure how long it would take you to get back from Southmoor. Would you rather I leave you alone?"

Alex shook his head. "No, it wouldn't hurt to have some company," he said, and pulled up another chair after bestowing a gentle kiss on Naomi's forehead.

"How was it?" Bill asked.

"It was more difficult than I'd anticipated," Alex replied, honestly. "I kept thinking of Naomi, and of Ian…but then, I thought of all the good work she'd done, as a detective over the years. I thought of Carl Deere again, and of the similarities between them."

"How so?"

"In his case, he was falsely accused, but became the monster in the end," Alex said. "In Ava's case, she made herself an instrument of vengeance but went far, far beyond her own boundaries when she attacked Ian and Naomi. She even admitted they weren't part of her plan."

"She was lucid, then?"

"Very," Alex replied, and thought back to their conversation. "It forced me to think of how blurred the lines of justice can be. Carl and Ava were both traumatised by events in their formative years, as I was. I find myself questioning whether my own path has been affected, more than I care to realise."

"You haven't killed anybody, that I know of," Bill said, with a smile.

"No, but I break the rules," Alex said. "I treated my own mother, when I knew it was forbidden. Porter wasn't wrong, when he chastised me for entering Daisy Richmond's flat without police backup; I shouldn't have helped Smythe and his bodyguard to break down the door, let alone enter, no matter what was at stake. It was outside my jurisdiction. As for Ava, I began by helping her, but ended up entrapping her."

He looked across at Naomi, and wondered if she could hear him.

"We both know that behaviour has a nasty tendency to escalate, if circumstances permit," he said, turning back to his friend, who continued to listen without judgment. "There's a darkness inside me, Bill. It's always been there. If I wanted to, I could unleash it, just as Ava did. It's why I can't bring myself to hate her, as I might have done otherwise."

Bill searched his face, and then nodded. "We all have darkness inside us," he said. "It's part of being human. We have impulses, good and bad, and it's a question of self-regulation. You've mastered that, over the years—never doubt your own strength because, I promise you, I don't. I have faith that you'll continue along the road you've chosen, because it's a good road."

Alex clasped his hands together. "I don't know what I'd do, if anything was to happen to Naomi," he said. "I worry that something would break, inside me; that self-regulation you're talking about, and the thing that keeps me on the right path. I'm not so very different to Ava, or Carl, and I know it, Bill. I *know* it, and I frighten myself."

Bill fell into a worried silence. "We'll have to distract you," he decided. "What you need is a meaty case to get your teeth stuck into."

"Has anything come through to the unit?"

Bill smiled. "As a matter of fact, it has."

The monitors continued to beep as the two men spoke of their next case, with Naomi asleep beside them, like a silent sentinel.

AUTHOR'S NOTE

As with all new characters, Dr Gregory has developed incrementally over the course of the past six books. He is, quite deliberately, an unfinished article; I see him as a man who strives to help others and, in doing so, helps to understand himself better, too. He is a character with a deep well of compassion for others, no matter their crime or ailment, which is an approach that the typical proponent of retributive justice may find difficult to reconcile but which is, I hope, interesting to read. I have always admired those who choose to dedicate themselves to helping others, especially within the realm of mental healthcare, where pain and suffering is not always visible. To go beyond that and see the worth of a human being who has committed untold acts of violence takes a very special kind of person, with an enormous capacity for understanding, and I have tried in my own way to channel this into the characters on these pages.

I hope you have enjoyed the latest outing of Gregory and Douglas; I'm looking forward to continuing their adventures!

Until the next time…

LJ ROSS
JULY 2024

Dr Alexander Gregory will return in...

OBSESSION

There's a thin line between obsession and madness...

With the woman he loves trapped in a coma, psychiatrist and criminal profiler Doctor Alex Gregory is starting to lose hope she'll ever come back to him. Desperate for a distraction, he takes on a new case at the behest of the Los Angeles Police Department.

It's a long way from home, but he agrees to profile whoever is responsible for sending threatening letters to a beautiful starlet Mia Mendoza, who's refusing to film her latest romantic comedy until the letters stop. It's putting the entire production in jeopardy, and Gregory is their last hope.

When things take a sinister turn, Gregory is forced to step inside the dark mind of a killer who will never, ever stop because it's more than just killing...

It's an obsession.

Available to order now!

LOVE READING?

JOIN THE CLUB...

Join the LJ Ross Book Club to connect with a thriving community of fellow book lovers! To receive a free monthly newsletter with exclusive author interviews and giveaways, sign up at www.ljrossauthor.com or follow the LJ Ross Book Club on social media:

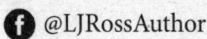 @LJRossAuthor

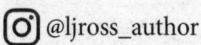 @ljross_author

ABOUT THE AUTHOR

LJ ROSS is an international bestselling author known for her atmospheric mystery and thriller novels, including the DCI Ryan series which has sold over 12 million copies worldwide. Her debut novel *Holy Island* published in 2015 and reached number one in the Amazon UK and Australian digital charts. Louise has since released over thirty novels, most of which have been UK number one digital bestsellers. She is also the creator of the bestselling Dr Alexander Gregory series and the Summer Suspense series. Louise is a keen philanthropist and proud to support numerous non-profit programmes in addition to founding the Lindisfarne Prize for Crime Fiction, the Northern Photography Prize and the Northern Film Prize.

Born in Northumberland, England, she studied Law at King's College, University of London, then abroad in Florence and Paris, and worked as a lawyer before pursuing her dream to write. She lives with her family in Northumberland.

If you would like to get in touch with LJ Ross on social media, please scan the QR code below – she would love to hear from you!

Have you read the rest of the Alexander Gregory thrillers by LJ Ross?

Atmospheric thrillers featuring forensic psychiatrist and criminal profiler Dr Alexander Gregory. Loved by readers for the fast-moving and page-turning plots, international locations and shocking twists, with psychology adding fascinating depth to the stories.

If you enjoyed this book why not try the bestselling DCI Ryan Mysteries by LJ Ross?

HOLY ISLAND

A DCI Ryan Mystery (Book 1)

Available to buy now!

Detective Chief Inspector Ryan retreats to Holy Island seeking sanctuary when he is forced to take sabbatical leave from his duties as a homicide detective. A few days before Christmas, his peace is shattered, and he is thrust back into the murky world of murder when a young woman is found dead amongst the ancient ruins of the nearby Priory.

When former local girl Dr Anna Taylor arrives back on the island as a police consultant, old memories swim to the surface making her confront her difficult past. She and Ryan struggle to work together to hunt a killer who hides in plain sight, while pagan ritual and small-town politics muddy the waters of their investigation.

Murder and mystery are peppered with a sprinkling of romance and humour in this fast-paced crime whodunnit set on the spectacular Northumbrian island of Lindisfarne, cut off from the English mainland by a tidal causeway.

Discover the international bestselling DCI Ryan series from LJ Ross

Atmospheric mysteries set amidst the spectacular landscape of the north east of England.

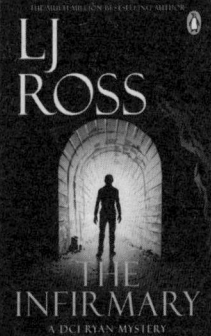

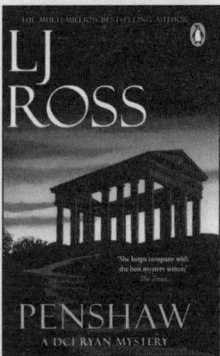

Discover the international bestselling DCI Ryan series from LJ Ross

Atmospheric mysteries set amidst the spectacular landscape of the north east of England.

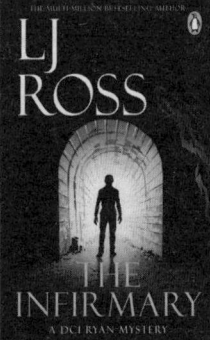

**Discover now the bestselling
Summer Suspense series from LJ Ross**

Suspense and mystery are peppered with romance and humour in these fast-paced thrillers set amidst the beautiful landscapes of Cornwall.

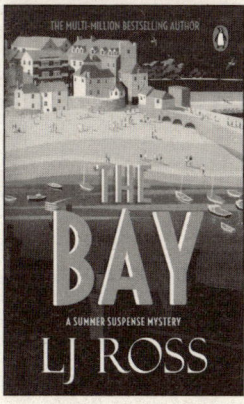